THEY WERE HERE BEFORE

KAREEN LOPEZ SAMUELS

Cadmus Publishing
www.cadmuspublishing.com

© 2020 Kareen Lopez Samuels
Cover art by Abigail Samuels

Published by Cadmus Publishing
www.cadmuspublishing.com

ISBN: 978-1-7343644-6-0
All rights reserved. Copyright under Berne Copyright Convention, Universal Copyright Convention, and Pan-American Copyright Convention. No part of this book may be reproduced, stored in a retrieval system, or transmitted in any form, or by any means, electronic, mechanical, photocopying, recording or otherwise, without prior permission of the author.

This is a work of fiction; therefore names, characters, places, and incidents are the products of the author's imagination or are used fictitiously. Any resemblance to actual events, locales, or persons, living or dead, is entirely coincidental.

THEY WERE HERE BEFORE

PROLOGUE

Legend has it that a Zulu prince fell insanely in love with a Shangana princess. They courted for a short while and everything was set for the jubilant celebration. However, the bride did not make an appearance on her wedding day. Rumours spread quickly that the girl's father had a change of heart and had sent her to live in the mountains among the ancient Oracles who protected her with their magic.

Obviously, this angered the Zulu king immensely who was forced to wage war against the Shangana people because pride and honour were at stake. Unfortunately, many innocent lives were lost and being naturally more aggressive, of course the Zulu tribe won. However, it was only a half-hearted victory because the real prize would have been the enchanting princess. Afterall, these two tribes had lived harmoniously for years and this union would have further cemented both their economic and political power in the region. Therefore, this rejection was substantial and an affront to the Zulus as was the unnecessary battle which ensued - a battle which significantly weakened their defenses and rendered them vulnerable to their enemies.

The princess never returned and the young prince aged rapidly and died in his prime of a broken heart. The death of the prince came as another huge blow to his people and obviously left a rift between the two tribes which previously traded their goods and supported each other's economy.

From that time until the present there has been a clear demarcation between the groups and this sad tale was passed on from generation to generation, through oral tradition, to ensure that this history would never be repeated. However, in the tradition of humanity, most of the details were lost as people could not remember the particulars of the narrative and it became a fable among the young but, the deep sense of loss and resentment became ingrained in their DNA. Even in modern times, the bitterness remains. In the process of time, people moved from city to city, town to town, tribe to tribe, clan to clan; almost forgetting where all the landmarks stand, all the while bearing the residue of this deep groaning in their soul. All the while missing the key message of the tale: to grow in love, rather than rushing in unwisely.

Chapter 1

Shaney

Shaney has always been both amazed and amused by people who claim to hate mornings. Really! How could anyone possibly hate mornings? When mornings are the very best part of any day. Well for her it always was and still is. It is always a time when she got to check her self and do her care routine; not just the usual: shower, brush teeth, etc. It is the time when she is able to unobtrusively check her aura.

She discovered a while back that she is an empath and being an empath has not been an easy journey for her. This means that she is as sensitive to emotions as a vampire is to light. Shaney has had to learn how to decipher energy. She has had to learn how to decode emotions. This literally means intentionally determining which emotions belong to her and which belong to the people around her. Invariably, this act of decoding sometimes leaves her drained.

So early each morning, she checks her mental state; analyze everything that is going on in her head and in her heart to be able to filter emotions as she goes through the day. Also, of necessity she has to have a handle on the people around her as well. Therefore, she does not make friends easily. It is hard enough with the few friends she already has; in that, she always knows how and what they are feeling. However, the why is often problematic. Clearly, both a blessing and curse to always be in touch with another person's burden. Some days it is as if she is executing Hercules' Twelve Labours all at once. However, she has learned to carry this load well. Lately, she almost never goes out on dates. She never meets up with anyone for coffee; ever. Any time she meets up with the few friends that she has, is always in a controlled environment. Well, actually there was that one time when she had gone to the Red Lobster on W 125th St. That however was a long time ago, when she had just moved from rural North Carolina; where the Great Smoky Mountains kiss the skyline and are always visible from almost every direction. The Great Smoky has framed her existence and it is a most picturesque backdrop to a laid-back existence.

Gazing out at the mountain range always gave her a sense of being grounded, cementing her existence in a sometime hostile world, along with a deep-seated tranquillity that she told herself, she would never encounter anywhere else. A load would instantly leave her shoulders and the tightness in her neck would ease just from making eye contact with the Great Mountain.

It does not matter what is going on in her life – mountains – no not just mountains - but trees, bodies of water, nature in general is always a balm for her, a natural escape from real life issues. If she were to ever experience a bad day, a day where she was grossly overwhelmed by the emotions of others; or her own, all she had to do was literally look to the hills and help would come by way of sweet peace.

This way of being has always defined her existence and as a child she convinced herself that there was a fairy, in those wide-open fields, hiding in trees, floating around in bodies of water who has just one job and that is to soothe her delicate emotions. Shaney even named her *Ruwa*. To this day, she doesn't even know what that word means, but one day, it just came to her – like a gift so she kept it.

Shaney moved to New York six years ago for a huge job opportunity; to work at an Advertising/Media company. It has been a dream come true, working with some of the most creative and talented people from all over the world. Going to work is like being a part of the UN, as each person on staff has been hand picked by a mysterious exec who values diversity above all else. She did not much care how or why she was selected; whether or not it was tokenism, the important thing is that she is here, sitting at tables, in rooms she could not even begin to imagine.

Of course, she had done some work in media, at a local station in

Charlotte as a behind the scenes crew member. While working at that news station, she had to commute everyday which was never pleasant. In retrospect, that was quite possibly the reason she had agreed to move to New York; little did she know at the time that New York City traffic is in a different league all together. This type of traffic is not just vehicular but there is also people traffic and sometimes pet traffic as well. That type of traffic is enough to destabilize all her seven Chakras for days; just too many angry people who are always in a hurry so they will step on or over you, they will push you down; but whichever way, they will get to their destination. Eventually, like so many others before her, she discovered that having a car in the Big Apple was a pointless luxury that she could gladly do without, thanks to the many and various Uber drivers.

She grew up in a tiny suburb of Gaston County called McAdenville, where things rarely changed and everyone knows everyone and nothing was private or sacred. For that exact reason and the fact that she felt like she was stifling she had to leave her small town. However, after she left her small town, she became aware that based on her genetic constitution New York was probably not the most ideal setting for her but by then it was too late to do anything about it. She often chastised herself for leaving peace and tranquility to live in a concrete jungle. From her little apartment in the city, as far as the eyes could see, all that exist is just concrete, some wood and fibreglass but mostly concrete. The reality is although she felt stifled in her small town; metaphorically, she came to observe that she could literally stifle to death from all the fumes in New York, not a lick of fresh air to be found anywhere. Why hadn't she done her research about living here? Why didn't anyone warn her?

Everyday she leaves her apartment is a frantic endeavour, a mad dash to be indoors, a way from the maddening crowds. She always felt like she was losing her breath then she would become painfully aware that she had been holding her breath for a while. The other issue is that, she would leave her apartment every morning, excited for all the possibilities and opportunities that a new day would bring, but by the time she returned home, she would be fighting a full-blown panic attack. How could she continue to live this way? This question was constantly on her mind and also why.

But as humanity has done for centuries, Shaney adjusted, adapted, assimilated and eventually evolved until she was vibing at a level that was more conducive to her delicate constitution. She learned to navigate her new world through various calming Apps and about a million nature rich images on her phone. She even got a few plants for her office and home. Also, because everything that sustains her is on her phone, she could constantly and consistently be found there. Her phone became her best friend and confidant; her happy place.

Far worst than crowded streets, the bane of her existence is the subway which she has to take at least twice a week round trip. She always had to brace herself for the violent onslaught of human emotions. Everything from extreme fear, pain, panic, anxiety to full blown rage and confusion. So many people are confused these days. Yes, the struggle is quite real for her. On those subway days, when she got home, it took her a lot longer to coax some amount of Zen back in her world and she would always wonder: how the hell did I get through today? Somehow, she always made it through each demanding day – Monday to Friday and then she would hit the repeat button. Indeed, she started to believe that a greater entity than her fairy was looking out for her; of course, she couldn't be entirely sure of what that entity is but it was comforting to know of such an existence in her world. Although she grew up attending Sunday School and taking part in other church activities; however, as the pressures of life became more intense, she attended church less and less until eventually church and everything it entails became a distant memory.

Also, when it comes to the issue of whether or not she believes in God, along with her political ideology, those are topics she prefers not to address. Afterall, it is no one's business what or whom she chooses to accept. Plus, those issues never came up with her very small circle of friends. Why bother to make things way more complicated than they need to be? She has learned that the quickest, the most reliable and certainly the most efficient way to rid yourself of friends is to discuss religion and politics. Obviously, her job entails discussing some amount of politics; as the saying goes, the personal most certainly is the political, but why would she take work home with her and spread it around her circle of friends. So yes, the jury is still out; in terms of her religious dogma, but she still likes to keep that door open by praying as often as she remembers. Also, she has made meditation a part of her regular care routine as she believes that meditating centres her, clears her mind and embodies a strong sense of Catharcism.

This morning being no different, she has been up since five and she always opens her windows as well to get a whiff of the crisp morning breeze (which seems quite fresh despite the setting) especially in the winter time. The winters are also problematic for Shaney, coming from a place with mild winters – little to no snow – to a place where they can get up to five feet of snow.

However, this morning as she opened her window, she seems to have let in some very unsettling energy but, at this point she is not concerned because this sometimes happens when she opens the window – nothing that a few moments of meditation couldn't chase a way.

Shaney launches into her meditation routine, at first just focusing on her blessings, then her most favourite inspirational quotes and finally her favourite Bible verse: Deuteronomy 8: 18 "…. for it is he that give thee the power to get wealth…". Wealth for her is not necessarily just money and assets but good health and blessings. But really, who is she kidding: why else would she leave serenity to live in chaos? At some point in our journey, as humans, the bag becomes an essential part of our blessings.

Unfortunately, this morning, none of those things helped to settle her, to ground her. Next, she turned to yoga but a few rounds of downward dog poses were proving inadequate to get her out of her feelings and out of her head.

Deflated, she showered and headed out to work as the busyness and routines of the day sometimes helped to distract her from her rumination.

Chapter 2

Nathan

Nathan loves his homeland. So many people have a very misguided understanding of the dark continent but he has never been happy living anywhere else. He has lived for brief periods in the U.K., the U.S., the South of France, visited the Caribbean; all thanks to his job. There's just no place like home – South Africa – well not the whole country, Port Elizabeth in the Eastern Cape. Eastern Cape is a relatively new Province, established in 1994. It was built on Xhosa land and he is a proud member of that clan. He was born in the small village of Graskop in the Province of Mpumalanga, but he has called the Cape home for many years now.

Nathan enjoys all the natural aspects of his homeland, but his most profound sense of pleasure comes from just visiting the many picturesque lakes in his country; his favourite being Lake Chrissie. This lake is known for its bird life, a fresh water lake that is fairly shallow. He has always been fascinated by large bodies of *ruwa* - water. The only problem is that he never learned how to swim. He has tried on many occasions; however, he always experiences a panic attack because no matter what he did, he always felt like he was drowning – just sinking into nothingness while being pulled in many directions. This particular difficulty always amuses his friends but he has never been able to fully express how genuinely traumatic this experience is for him. After a while, he never thought much of his inability to swim and he agrees with his friends' conclusion, that he just needed to grow a strong stomach. But he takes comfort in the fact that he has a benevolent heart for everything else.

    He has been home for a while, as he has not been sent on any out of country projects by the Advertising company that he works with for a while now, which suits him just fine; no place like home. Despite all the hardships and political upheavals that his people have endured and maybe for that very reason, a sense of nationalism is entrenched in his psyche. Afterall, look at what's going on in the US, dear God, they are going through the Trump years. They can keep him, no two ways about that. Nathan feels like he is finally in a good place as he can see clear signs of upward mobility in his job; especially, in a world where job security is an ongoing issue. As a matter of fact, he lives by the following mantra, "In any moment we have two options: Step forward into GROWTH, or backwards to safety." Nathan, has always been determined to move forward regardless of the many obstacles he has faced. He never accepts defeat and reminds himself constantly that a growth mindset and grit is all he needs to navigate this sometimes-unsympathetic world.

Chapter 3

Shaney

Despite all the foreboding, Shaney got herself together, managed to fight through the people traffic and got to work with time to spare before the daily huddle. Needless to say, that this congregating is always perturbing for her but the fact that it's a quick gathering helps.

Naturally, having a little extra time means a quick visit to her Instagram (IG) account. For someone who is quite anti-social, Shaney really loves Social Media (S.M.) and really who can blame her? Social Media brings people from all races, class and creed together; and is therefore, an opportunity to live vicariously through others: go to places she would never be able to go, meet new people, fall in love, break up with them over the span of a few posts and never leave the comfort of her home or office. Regular people get to see celebrities up close and personal, and observe what life is like in other parts of the world. Through this medium, she gets to explore the human condition as she is given an insight into how connected we all are as individuals, how similar we all are, the various emotions that we all experience and this is on display through people's lived experiences. Of course, some of it is staged but who really cares, when it is a free source of entertainment and a free way to connect.

Speaking of which, clicking from one post to the next, Shaney has discovered someone who seems to be quite similar to her except that he is an extrovert, not an introvert like her; although, it is hard to tell, he could really be an ambivert. His name is *LuanMelokuhle*. She is well

THEY WERE HERE BEFORE

aware that this might not be his real name but after a quick Google search she concurs that this name suits him quite well because it literally means; "Lion stand up for good". This name suits him not only because his profile picture is an image of a lion but also because of his stance and understanding of notions around social justice; but also, because, he seems to possess a deeply insightful understanding of the human condition. This core understanding can not be faked it would have had to emerge from a life well lived, a life that has embraced a specific kind of suffering which has left the individual better and not bitter. Luan strongly favours unity for all African nations but even in that call for unity; he still celebrates the uniqueness of those individual nations.

Last month, he went on a two-week rant, calling out the hypocrisy of African leaders for their seeming nonchalance as it relates to the plight of their people, some of whom still living in deplorable conditions, in townships like Soweto. Needless to say, because Soweto is important to him, it is also important to her, that's just how it is; therefore, she did a Google search and made this startling discovery about Soweto.

Soweto was created in the 1930s when the white government started separating blacks from whites, creating black "Townships". Black people were separated from whites by a so called "cordon sanitaire" which was usually a river, railway track, industrial area or highway.

She was in shock and awe because this was clearly another way of separating and segregating people based fundamentally, not on war crimes or any such thing but based on skin colour. This discovery resonates with her own history in particular the Jim Crow Laws which was legislated by parliament and practised all the way up to 1965. As a matter of cold fact, the sanitary corridor was just the precursor to Apartheid in South Africa. This was the most systemic and lasting form of racism because it was entrenched in the institutions which were supposed to serve humans but turned out to be the delivery systems to perpetuate hate against a specific segment of humanity.

Luan often times, decries the poor social conditions which still exist in Soweto: sometimes he seems frustrated, other times enraged and a few times confused. Yes, she can read tone in images and words as well with or without exclamation marks. Sometimes she understands vibes even before a single word is expressed, even more so than words. The situation in Soweto is deeply disturbing. Shaney thought, like, wow, Black people can't catch a break, not even in their own country.

After these disturbing discoveries, I desperately want to reach out to my lion king to let him know that I am with him and I am for him; however, I am just way too shy. Plus, what if he rejects me? I have a panic attack every time I attempt to click the little heart to turn it red. That little heart is a symbol of my love for my king of the jungle. No, I absolutely could never try to get his attention. I have this irrational fear that if I ever liked one of his posts, then his attention would be drawn to my own very boring, therapy posts. All I post are: images of flowers, a variety of trees, bodies of water, a wide assortment of animals and "woke" quotes which speak to me at a deep level. Unlike other people's, my IG is dedicated primarily to my emotional well being which I absolutely need if I am going to continue to live in New York City. At this point, I have fifty followers and I am quite sure they follow me out of a deep sense of sympathy. Also, I thank my fairy that Mr. Luan's account is not private, which would have required me to send a "follow request" and would require him to allow me to be a follower. That would be an absolute disaster. What if he rejects me? This rejection has happened before and it took me months to even log into IG again; as a matter of cold fact, I almost deleted my account.

The precursor to this happened that one time when I had recently moved to New York and I met a guy in Red Lobster. I forced myself out of a sense of loneliness to sit there and talk with him for forty-five minutes. The longest forty-five minutes of my life. Anyways, at the end, I didn't want to exchange numbers so we exchanged Social Media information but he did not tell me that his account is private. Normally, I would not have been so brazen as to send him a friend request but since we had had such a, well, interesting conversation, I felt like it would be safe enough to do so. However, after I sent that request, I stayed online for almost two hours waiting on him to accept and when he didn't, I felt like I was going to die. I was crushed! Thankfully, there is a cancel request option and since that time, I have never made that mistake again, nor would I ever attempt anything so dangerous again.

THEY WERE HERE BEFORE 13

Nope, way too stressful!

I continue to enjoy this one-way transaction with the Nemean Lion. This is another term of endearment as he seems impervious to other people's scathing comments. For instance, there was that time when he had posted a comment about Donald J Trump and half his over two hundred thousand followers lost their minds. It was horrible to watch. I felt every blow delivered by each scalding tirade. It was way too much for me emotionally, I went to bed feeling chafed and raw. But true to form, the Lion king was in his element and he took on the most ferocious of his attackers. In fact, the next day he posted a gorgeous picture of himself, dressed in full black and as a pre-emptive strive, his caption read "My Haters Have Arrived". The Lion is always in fine form and hilarious beyond measure. That is the other thing I love about him, his sense of humour and how he is able to use it with skilful agility to deflate his attackers.

Some days, I sit in silent reverence envisioning the conversations that we could have and the lascivious deeds that would follow. Over and over again, I catch myself grinning from ear to ear, in private pleasure gained from these salacious reckonings; while also blushing at the same time. These escapades would emerge in my mind at the most incongruous times. It is sometimes cringe worthy; especially, moments when people would catch me smiling for no reason that's apparent to them. The shame is real but the pleasure greater; therefore, I can not come up with a good enough reason to cease and desist. Clearly, I can do whatever I please in the confines and solitude of my own mind which I do often despite sometimes feeling like I am dreaming my whole life away, living my whole life in someone else's world.

However, I find comfort in knowing that some people play leading roles while others pay to watch. I do get depressed sometimes by this very meagre, subsistent existence but how can I ever imagine living any other way when living in my head for a life time, being all I know. How can a person change without knowing of another way of being? One can not change what they can't see.

Chapter 4

Shaney - The Huddle

It seems like I have been in a dreamlike state for hours when my team leader – Michael – called us together for the usual lacklustre meeting. So, I braise myself for his monotone over the next fifteen minutes which would invariably creep by on snail legs.

Thankfully, not today. Today, Michael is upbeat and excited. After a few minutes I pull myself away from my private session, as this meeting seems important so I didn't want to miss anything, just in time for Michael to exclaim, "Our most recent client wants to expand their business worldwide". I thought, wow, that's awesome! That means we are doing well at our location. He continues, "They want us to send a team on a fact-finding mission. Therefore, we are in the process of selecting two individuals from here and they will choose one from South Africa". I thought, they would never pick me, not in a million years.

Someone asks the question that is at the forefront of my mind. "So where in the world are we going on this fact-finding mission?" I absolutely do not need to look around to discover who the voice is. It is the new girl who recently joined our team, her aura is always intense and she is always overly vivacious: she mostly reminds me of Ms. Fine from The Nanny. This girl is so damn fake! Everything about her; from her nails, to her smile, to her eyelashes, all store bought. The only thing organic about her is her beautiful mane, natural and vibrant hair, just like mine. I don't really mind the fact that she is always so bubbly but this personality type is sometimes quite overwhelming for me to the

THEY WERE HERE BEFORE 15

point where I didn't quite get her name when she was first introduced. This sometimes happens during introductions, I get distracted by a particular quality in a person, I zone out and before you know it I miss important information, such as names. Therefore, I named her Glow which I am always careful not to say aloud. Also, it comes as no surprise that Glow has said, "we". She always does this, find a way to insert herself into every discussion, every opening, every new opportunity, every striking thing. She is the type of girl who is so driven that she drives people away. There is no question that she will be going on this mission.

Eventually, Michael declares that, "The client wants the team to start in South Africa". All of a sudden without thinking, without overthinking, without practising my response multiple times in my head, without considering tone, resonance or implications; I do something that I have never done before. I said in a really, rushed, breathy voice,

"Michael, seeing that I am African American can I go to South Africa?"

I am flabbergasted at myself and based on all the bewildered expressions in the room, so is everyone else. Everyone, that is, except Michael, he responds with a huge smile,

"Shan, we were actually hoping that you would volunteer, well… ahh… not for that reason though. It is because of your attention to details and your vast experience in that area".

Yes, Shan is my team name which I really don't mind because it carries a sense of belonging and comradery. I actually started telling my family members to call me Shan, this of course mortified my mom because she is one who chose Shaney.

Invariably, I am beside myself and I am being assuaged by a tremendous amount of emotions but they will have to wait until later to sort them into various files: mine/not mine, keep/delete. Imagine, walking into my day, thinking it was going to be same old same old and then voila, I am a member of the team going to South Africa to make new discoveries, all expense paid and get paid on top of that. I love my job!

Suddenly, I feel myself come to life, a very visceral reaction; like an awakening, a renewal even. So much so, that my shoulders straighten and I feel about two feet taller; if that is even possible. Unexpectedly, there's a newly acquired knowledge in me that all my living, all my mistakes, all my missteps, all my failings, all my accomplishments, all my passions, all my pain, all my flaws have brought me to this moment, this moment when I come into myself. A moment when my life is about to change, a moment when my life is about to finally make sense. A momentary shift in the trajectory of my life that will wrench me out of self preservation mode and lasso me into my destiny, my purpose. Imagine that, finally waking up into my own life; my own personal Matrix.

Chapter 5

Shaney

When I get home that evening, I anticipate an avalanche of tormenting emotions, but none make an appearance. As a matter of fact, all day at work, on my way home in my Uber, I wait and search deep inside myself for them but no such devil assails me. I had to reprimand myself for being worried about not being worried.

After a mandatory wash, to get rid of other people's germs, I had a quick supper of left-over greens, baked chicken and mac and cheese. I am even sick of having the same kind of food all the time. Anyways, since I am having a Zen moment, I could go visit my internet friend. Also, I feel a burst of confidence, so possibly, maybe, just maybe tonight is the night I might be able to double click on the little heart - under one of his hundreds of posts - and watch it turn red. Wouldn't that be spectacular! I smile conspiratorially.

Haphazardly, I click on Luan's followers and instantly ushered into a world of lush, green foliage. A world I didn't even know existed prior to meeting this amazing man. I figured that since it is a done deal and by all intents and purposes, I am going on this trip, I might as well learn about the place that I would be spending the next ninety days of my life. We actually discovered today that since we are US citizens, we did not need to get a Visitor's Visa, if we only stay for three months; however, if our situation changes and we need to stay longer we could go online and request an EVisa. On the other hand, my Lion would need to have a US Visa to come and visit me which does not seem right, not at all. But oh well, the joys of capitalism, I guess South Africa doesn't have anything that we currently need right about now. Decidedly, three months would be more than enough time to do our research, explore and submit our reports. Of course, Glow is going as well and it makes sense since she is African American as well; regardless, of what Michael said in the meeting. But who cares?

I turn on my iPad and go to my downloads, just for some background music. One of my all-time favourite songs come on immediately. "I had the time of my life and I owe it all to you….". Could this song be prophetic? I hope so!

Anyways, I guess there are far worse travel partners than Glow and who knows we might even become friends. I laugh out loud at that idea. Who am I kidding? I am technically the type of person who prefers to live in her head rather than live in the real world. For instance, I am the type of crazy who will see, not even meet, but just see a guy at the mall or online and start making plans for our wedding: choose the colours, the venue, the honeymoon location and name our children, all in the space of a few hours. Also, generally I am an expert at picking the most emotionally unavailable men, which is ironic since I am the vibe queen. In the past, I have had a total of two relationships and although the guys seemingly are different; essentially, emotionally they are the very same. Which is why these days, I am a lot more introverted than before so I just go to work, come home and get my fix from IG. I already have more than enough issues, I don't need anyone to add to my growing list. This is something I have come to accept about myself; consequently, consistently sparkling Glow would never be interested in cultivating a friendship with someone who is as bland as myself. She always seems to be on the prowl for stimulation and I am the greatest sedative ever! Plus, her vivacious vibrancy would be way too oppressive for me, she would absolutely suffocate me. So, no, we are totally incompatible! There is no way we could become friends, not now, not ever!

With a sigh, I continue to click on follower after follower and witness the most tantalizing landscapes that I have ever seen. Not to detract from the Great Smoky, but their brilliance renders the

Great Smoky, Pale Smoky in comparison. Image after image presents picture perfect, post cards of: low areas, raised areas, primal browns, vibrant greens, little streams, sturdy boulders, gregarious animals, varying blue hues dapple the sky which provides an opulent backdrop to the vast beauty of this land mass. Additionally, there are many cascading waterfalls which sparkle much like resplendent jewels decorating a Rubenesque princess.

It was at this precise moment, I wish that I had paid closer attention in English class as I discovered that I lacked the words to describe such a rich oasis. Although I believe that even the great Shakespeare and even Chaucer himself would have struggled to articulate the most fitting and appropriate words to fully describe this elaborate expanse which is Africa in general but South Africa in particular. All the natural remedy to soothe my troubled soul. Imagine searching for a cure and not knowing the cure was readily available all along.

People can say all they want about S. M. but I am grateful for it. How else would I have discovered so many new places, made so many new friends; friends I don't even have to talk with, entertain or go out with. Let's face it, how many people are able to afford expensive trips? Not that many right but through this medium we are able to visit far away locations, do research based on sound bites and images from across the globe. The world is indeed a global village; after all, it does take a village and we are all children of the world.

Invigorated by the artistic renderings of the Master painter, I plough deeper and deeper into the underbelly of the internet; totally and utterly amazed by the candor of the people here. They seem to have carved out a safe space for themselves to express wide-ranging opinions on various topics, everything from the intellectual, the political, to the hypothetical, the strongly emotional, to the very fundamental and all shared with an undertone of humour. I love it here!

On my quest, I come across a phrase that greatly resonates with me, at my most vulnerable and primal level: "We Are Our Ancestors' Wildest Dreams". Wow! This gets me thinking about my lineage; but in truth and in fact, I have never thought about anyone in my family beyond my grand parents. I am not from a family that shares oral history and familial stories. We don't even talk about genetic sicknesses and diseases so I'm not even sure where to begin in terms of processing this new ideology.

One thing I know for sure, is the fact that we are African Americans more than implies that our origin started in Africa but where in Africa is the big mystery. Africa is such a colossal continent, well to me it is. When you come from such a relatively small place – McAdenville and a State that is just 139, 390 square kilometres compared to 30.37 million square kilometres there is virtually no comparison. Essentially, not even the great State of New York, the Big Apple can be compared to Africa. There are so many diverse tribes or clans (I learnt this from my IG friends) peoples, customs, beliefs, practises, in general, Africa and Africaness is such an enigma that it is indeed both daunting and terrifying to conceptualize. The half has never yet been told is an understatement. Evidently, that number does not take into consideration the diasporas of the Americas, the Caribbean and other places where Africans were dropped off or have decided to populate.

As expected, overtime the inordinate nature of my thinking and the vivid images begin to weigh heavily on me so I reluctantly call it a night. Even the very images themselves speak to me so forcefully, they bear an emotional intelligence which is both inspiring and draining.

All at once, this trip is starting to prove far more significant than I initially thought. But I am still secure in my desire to go even though as usual, my overthinking has basically terrified me beyond measure and now I am inordinately scared and super anxious (in a good way). However, I am still beyond thrilled to go: to meet new people, to learn new things, to make new discoveries about myself and potentially about my genealogy; where my bloodline comes from, where all my idiosyncrasies come from. Some people say that we should not live in the past and I quite agree but being a square peg in a round world is quite isolating and confusing at times. Needless to say, sometimes we have to examine the past, to clarify the present and extricate the future because clearly without knowledge of the past we run the risk of making the same blunders as our fore parents.

THEY WERE HERE BEFORE

Plus, I am sick and tired of being sick and tired and of feeling stuck like I am going around in circles. Imagine, knowing you are badly broken and in search of someone, anyone or something to fix you, but having the power in you to heal yourself all along but not being aware of that power. Also, not having the keys to unlock that power. Yes, maybe going to my people will make me whole again.

Chapter 6

Shaney

It is true what they say, that life moves in leaps and bounds and never has this ever been more applicable to my life than right now. Essentially, I go from having an existential crisis, from feeling like I am stifling, to walking into the opportunity of a life time. However, as thrilled as I am, I am a little disturbed by a dream that I had last night. But the problem is, I can not bring back the details to the foreground of my mind. The images are still there, I can sense them. I can also sense that these images want to converse with me but something in my consciousness keeps blocking them and I have an annoying itch to just reach into my mind and yank them forward.

The aspect that I do remember is me drowning, or choking, definitely suffocating but the whole thing lacks context. There are a lot of people around me, gaping in fear, people I don't recognize but they are there and I am drowning and no one is attempting to save me. The absence of a frame of reference quickly place that frame into oblivion. Drowning could actually be speaking to overwhelming emotions but outside of that broad category I have no way of solidifying my understanding of the dream. It could also mean that no one is coming to save me and that I need to save myself. So utterly frustrating!

It frustrates me to not be able to call back the dream. I am even more off kilter because of the residue of the dream which haunts me but forbids me to hold on to the substance of it as well. I desperately try to push the dregs of the dream aside because today is not the day to be out of focus. I have so many things to do: renew my passport, clean my house and my office, get some shopping done and train the person who will be filling in for me. I genuinely do not have time for this distraction right now.

    All the negativity of the dream aside, I did not realize that this trip and all the possibilities that go along with it, is exactly what my soul has been craving. Of late, I have had the deepest yearning and a desperate need for newness, for a regenesis; so much so that I don't even know, if this novelty that I seek even exist in any physical plane. I have been yearning for deep conversations with people of substance rather than the superficial blather which passes for meaningful discussion. This change of scenery is going to be therapeutic for me, I can already sense it in all the systems of my body. Who knows, life is funny sometimes, I might actually meet my Lion. Clearly, that is outside the realm of human possibility but who knows, we might just bump into each other in the marketplace. Oh well, a girl can hope can she not! My intuition is pointing to an epiphany and I am ready for it with bated breath.

Chapter 7

Nathan

"Hey Nathan, I have an assignment for you".

"What is it?"

"Some Americans will be visiting for a fact-finding mission and they are in need of a local guide".

"Okay, that's fine".

"Don't you want to hear what they are going to investigate?"

"Sure, that would be useful information!"

"They work for a Media company which represents various clients and apparently one of their clients is looking to expand and include South Africa in their portfolio".

"That's excellent! More work for locals and a boost to the economy. That's a win and a win in my book. I will be happy to assist".

"Oh, by the way, you will have to stay in Pretoria. They've already booked a hotel there to be closer to the American Embassy just in case anything goes wrong and we didn't want to ask them to cancel. Also, because Pretoria is a safe place, that is probably best for them to stay there".

"Yeah, that's fine. I'm flexible! Plus, as you say, we will be traveling a lot so it might be best to be near Joburg. We can also use our local offices there, to do the administrative stuff".

"Okay, great! I will inform them at the Johannesburg office, it's a good thing we didn't sell it when we moved offices. We'll book you in a hotel close to theirs. I figured you would like to keep things separate".

THEY WERE HERE BEFORE 25

"Again, I'm flexible".

"Thanks Nathan! I knew you were the best man for the job".

Nathan had this conversation with his immediate supervisor and despite his outward show of optimism, found that he was a little annoyed that he had been selected for the special job of being a tour guide without his consent. Because, he is the "best man for the job". *EISH!* (RUBBISH) He thought, why? Is it because I am the only Black South African working here? What do they take me for, a bushman? I will definitely find a way to uncover why I was selected. There is always a reason and sometimes it is not as grandiose as they would have you think.

Clearly, the decision has already been made; therefore, I will just accept that it is, for the good of the cause, as Descartes said, "The greatest good for the greatest number". Also, it is apparent that all my responsibilities have been shelved so there is nothing to do for the next few days while I await the *abafikayos* - outsiders. That is quite amendable to me. In the meantime, I will make myself more conversant with American culture. Mind you, American ideology is all around me; after all, everyone knows about America through her movies, news, fast food franchises and clothing brands. You know that you have attained some measure of success once you are able to buy American. In deed, America is still a super power despite their current immigration policies. She has her tentacles in every nook and cranny of the world and has managed to permeate the landscape of our understanding, defining what it means to be successful in the world.

Today, I will start my research on IG. As a matter of fact, I will start with my most recent follower: ShanShan_icclearly – whatever that means. People are so funny! They come up with the most obscure screen names. Anyways, if it brings them joy, who am I to judge! She seems really, as the Americans say, "cool". Oh yes, I will have to learn their many slangs as well. For that, I will most definitely need more than a few days to learn their many *isaladi* (idioms). They are a people who are dead set on changing the world, one word, one vowel, one consonant, one phrase at a time. I will need to check the Great Oracle Google before attending to Shan Shan's profile to become a breast of American slangs. I have not been there in years and they put out new slangs everyday, much like music and movies.

Shan seems big into nature, she would definitely enjoy South Africa; with our naturally beautiful landscapes and scenery. Let's see, she has one pic of herself looking all Zen as they would say. She doesn't really say much, so I don't know what social issues she feels strongly about. I hate how some Americans choose to be so *ukungazi* – ignorant - of the world's problems. It is as if they choose to live in a bubble, not a care in the world. Needless to say, the world looks to them to create solutions for most of the problems that they have helped to create. That being said, it must be nice to be so far removed from the maladies which plague the rest of humanity; primarily, developing nations. Meanwhile, a luta continua in places where freedoms have been denied for so long and people are still in the process of carving out a niche for themselves and their families. I guess they see these as third world problems.

Nevertheless, as annoyed as I am, there is something captivating about Ms. Shan Shan, although she seems to be hiding herself; but the more she seems far removed from the world, is the more appealing she emerges. In contrast to people who put everything out there: butt, breasts, belly, meals, relationship issues, all their life on public display. Come to think of it, I guess it must be quite liberating to not give a shit about what people think of your most uncomely parts. We all have to admit that Americans are trendsetters in the era of: #selflove, #selfcare and my personal favourite #blackgirlmagic which seems to mean, give as much advice as you can fit in a single post. Americans are amusing! Plus, what in thunderation is Black girl magic, which magician supplies that? How come it is only Black girls who have this magic? It is never Black men, or girls from other ethnicities? Don't they have magicians? I have questions.

I soon realize that I have spent quite a long time on Shan's profile. I quickly scan others that seem American but some how I always seem to be yanked back to her profile, looking at the solitary image of her, like a lone some dove; with a mountain range at her back, eyes closed in silent meditation and her hands raised in gratitude. I wonder which State she is from. A Google search brings me to the Great Smoky mountain range. Okay, she is from North Carolina or Tennessee, a country girl, by all indications. She would be at complete peace in our most alluring country.

Chapter 8

Nathan

In the blink of an eye, Nathan is booked in a hotel in Pretoria, awaiting his charges. He settles in, and spends more time online to discover as much as he can about life in America. However, since he discovered Shan Shan, she is present in all his waking moments, a fixture in his life. Also, having time on his hands, he engrosses himself in the affairs of America as he feels like this will help to make conversing with his guests more organic; as it is so easy to have misunderstandings and make assumptions when words mean different things, to different people.

After being online for some time, Nathan decides to grab some lunch, he was in the mood for biltong and some bunny chow. He kept wondering if Shan would enjoy the ethnic cuisines his country serves up so readily or the hustle and bustle of the busy market. He had to laugh at himself. How could he be so *verslaan* (smitten) with a girl he doesn't even know (*weet*)? But for some reason, he just could not get her out of his head. This obsession (for the lack of a better word) being so infinitely out of character for him that he started to wonder if he had been bewitched. He found himself wondering if a jealous spirit had somehow taken hold of his mind, with a view to distract him from his job. This idea seems so improbable but it could happen and it has happened. Mind you, Nathan has never been one to give any credence to old wife's fables but this sudden attack, this unprecedented assault (*aanval*) – again, for the lack of a more precise term, seems so invasive and aggressive. A quick check of the facts in the situation reveals: he an educated man (the most educated in his family) being obsessed with an American woman, eighteen hours away by plane, in a different time zone; essentially, half the world away, who doesn't know him, his many languages or the ways of his people. For multiple and obvious reasons, this does not make any good sense. More to the point then, he must be bewitched because how else could one explain this intrusive phenomenon.

As a matter of hard fact, he vaguely remembers that a boy from his village – in Graskop – who somehow managed to escape the drudgery of village life, having won a full scholarship; however, lost it after the first year because he had fallen madly in love with a coloured girl. Madly, being the operative word as it was used to describe him often because that was definitely insanity, there was just no other way to describe his sudden predicament. The truth is, in South Africa and other African nations, just developing nations in general, not many people get to abscond village life or life in the townships. It is generally an undeclared rule, that whatever your circumstances are at the time of your birth, those circumstances very rarely change until death and then children are born, live this way, die this way and the cycle continues. Naturally, everyone in the village had agree, that it must have been one of the other candidates who had not received the prestigious scholarship who must have been so angry and jealous that he had evoked a jealous spirit in the life of poor Mabuti (yes, that was his name). Afterall, how else could an intelligent boy lose something so precious and love be blamed for it? Love is not foolish, no she is wise and of a sound mind. Nathan has never fully grasped the meaning of the phrase, *love makes fools of the wise* because; clearly, they must have been fools to begin with. So, no, love can not be held in contempt for the actions of fools. For the villagers, there was just absolutely no other way to explain this folly; other than witchcraft, as it goes against all that is logical and falls outside the realm of human comprehension. Inevitably, everyone had to concede that Mabuti had been cursed. Sadly, since then, he has not been seen or heard from again and obviously if he did return, the elders would have to ask him to leave for the good of the commune; after all, he had been touched by *Tekkies* (evil spirits). Per adventure, his presence in the village would lead to way too many complications so it is definitely in everyone's best interest that he never returns.

Nathan, manages to snap himself out of his uncanny reflection and shake his head from side to side to banish any lingering malicious ideas. He then quickly surveills his immediate environs to see if there was anyone looking at him suspiciously, to some how spot the source of his very vivid imaginings. But alas, there was no one that he was close enough to identify the mischief in his or her face. Again, he shakes his head to both quiet and reject any other forbidden notions seeking to lodge in his mind, to entrap him, give birth and multiply into a cacophony of insanity. Because after all, isn't that usually how insanity begins; with just a thought?

Just when I thought I was losing it for sure; suddenly, a face appears in front of me and it pulls me out of my stupor. It is the face of my aunt (*Tante*) Toishma, my mom's eldest and quite eccentric sister. She looks at me in a peculiar way. Then eventually, figuring that I have not gone mad, tentatively says, "*Heita*" by way of greeting. So, I responded in kind, "Hello tante. How are you? *Sanibonani*". Aunt Toishma declares, "*Dit gaan goed met my suide*!" "I am quite happy to hear that you are fine tante". We make small talk for a while - which we both hate - but based on our surroundings there is no room for anything more substantial.

Of all my mom's siblings and relatives, I have always preferred Toishma because of her candor, her fortitude and strength of character. Lore has in it our family that, she was once married to a man from a different clan (which is unusual in itself because our clan is exogamous) who moved her to his village and treated her like a slave. On top of that, his village did not have a lot to offer in terms if scenery. The landscape was dry and consisted of mostly boulders and dried grass, which did not bode well with my aunt's personality. She is the kind of person who needs constant stimulation from nature: the trees, the streams, birds, flowers. Eventually, she did manage to escape her captor and start a new life for herself and her two children. Also, at a time when divorce and remarriage was frowned upon and therefore met with social isolation; she beseeched the elders to consider her case, this she did so frequently and so passionately that eventually they had to acquiesce to her demands. She later decided to marry another man from another clan; however, she convinced him to live with her in our village. Now whether or not they are living their happily ever after, no one can say for sure. In fact, I once asked her if she was happy and her response was,

"My *umtshana*, that is the problem with today's generation, everyone wants to be happy. Why must everyone be happy? Why is happiness so highly valued above all other virtues when there are far more honourable ways of being".

I did not ask what that meant because I did not want to get into a fight with her. I know for sure that I would never win. But I keep wondering what could be more worthy than to be happy? What goal is more noble than to attain to a level of Zen that makes one unavailable to the human condition to which we are all prone, by virtue of birth?

Aunt Toishma's word is definitely plausible since she has undoubtedly overcome profound hardships and has come out on the other side wiser, kinder and stronger. She is deeply empathetic, never judgmental and always quick to help. She once told me that, "hardship is the mother of virtue, because suffering is never random but suffering makes us infinitely more human and more perceptive of the human condition". She is always quick to remind us that, "God is not a slave master and he takes no pleasure in inflicting pain. Also, pain is a matter of perspective as it depends on how you choose to perceive pain; therefore, it has the potential to make you bitter or better, more or less human". She told me that she always chooses to be better and more human, always evolving, becoming a better version of herself. As a matter of fact, the most radical thing she has ever said is, "Always try to stay in touch with the ancestors and God will use them to help you on your quest to be better". Those are very deep and scary suppositions right there, way too advance for me. How can the living and the dead co-exist? Are the ancestors considered angels? However, despite my deep desire to know more I fully did not pursue any more communication in this regard, on that topic, neither did I think about what that might mean. I have come to accept that in this life there are ideas that are far above my ability to comprehend. And I have fully embraced this notion so I have actually made peace with my level of ignorance. The complete irony though, considering that I am the educated one.

That being said, on this very confusing day, under the piping hot sun, being so overcome with emotions; I decide to move to a more secure location to have a heart to heart with my favourite aunt. Thankfully, she was in town today to do her weekly shopping because she had missed her ride the previous day and could not muster the energy for the five hours commute that she would have had to make otherwise. As she keeps saying, *all things truly work together for good*. This was a stroke of luck for me because I really need help and guidance in deciphering all these complex emotions and who best to serve up some wisdom than my most trusted family member. I really needed to hear words of wisdom on a day like today.

Chapter 9

Shaney

I feel like I am walking in a daze, wide awake in a dream. It took us eighteen hours to get here and it was worth every second of discomfort on that cramped flight. I am so overjoyed that I barely remember the flight. This must be exactly how mother's feel when they look at their newborn for the first time: they forget the malaise of the pregnancy and the anguish of delivery. Even Glow didn't bother me much on the flight. I actually made an effort to learn her name - as it turns out my name is better – her name is way too ordinary for her flamboyance.

We land at Johannesburg International Airport to the rhythm of a torrential downpour but by the time our Uber arrives it has stopped and the air is breathtakingly fresh. The air feels like it has been filtered and purified; just for us, definitely a clear sign of a welcome, an embrace even. You know how we always clean our house in anticipation of an important visitor. I perceive this as a good omen which lifts my already elevated spirits as I was vibing at an unusually high level. Also, when the lady at customs said, "*Sanibonani*" with a huge smile, I felt that deeply. I am not sure why just yet but I just do.

We are booked to stay in the *Protea* Hotel in Pretoria about thirty-three miles from Johannesburg, a condominium inspired building with all the modern amenities which I have come to love. Glow and I share the unit and we have all the amenities of modern living: free Wi-Fi, huge rooms, comfortable furnishing, two bedrooms, a kitchenette, living and dining area and a good size bathroom. It really did not feel like a visit, it felt like a home away from home; I feel like I am home, like I had travelled all my life to return home. Back home in North Carolina we have a house - well my parents have a house – but when I moved to New York I live in a condo so I got accustomed to the convenience of a condo. Therefore, this set up for the next three months suits me just fine.

Our unit is extremely clean, not a single bed bug in sight; apparently, Glow has a phobia. The best part is that from our room, we have a spectacular view of the city. Surprisingly, Pretoria is undeniably a modern city, with all the fanfare but without the huge wall of cement. I can still see magnificent trees interspersed among the buildings. Our room is bright with tons of natural light from the huge balcony and three substantial windows. Trees, natural light, fresh air, I am in my natural habitat. There is also an office suite with computers all neatly organized to reflect the modern office, a swimming pool (get this, a rooftop swimming pool) outdoor patio for dining, just absolutely amazing décor everywhere. Clearly, whoever designed and built this hotel had me in mind. That being said, this property has seen better days and to the super finicky it would be problematic but not for me: I am finally home.

The next day, I am anxious to take a look around the city so I get up early as usual and go for a stroll – I don't wander too far from our building – before our local guide arives. It doesn't even bother me that no one came to meet us at the airport. Glow has been livid since last night. Oh well, whatevs! I am accustomed to doing my own thing without any guidance or supervision and I actually enjoy the freedom to choose my own schedule and go at my own pace, be a tourist for at least a few days.

On my early morning stroll, I come across the most glorious trees I have ever seen in my life. They are purple, there is a sea of purple as far as the eye can see, mind you, purple has never been one of my favourite colours but this tree – the Jacaranda tree – is breathtakingly impressive. Interestingly, I discover that Johannesburg is home to the largest man-made urban forest in the world, well maybe one of the largest. I also discover a flowering plant which I have never seen before, Lobostemon Fruticosus, endemic to South Africa and has over thirty varieties and many colours but I mostly see baby blue and light pink. Trees, lush vegetation, I couldn't ask for a more perfect spot. However, poor Glow is not faring so well – allergies.

    Later that day, we meet up with a team from the local company that we will be in partnership with. They apologise profusely for not having anyone meet us at the airport. They also said that our local guide (and third team member) had been called away on urgent, family business and would be back the following day. In the meantime, they brought us up to speed on the areas that we would be covering on this trip. I could listen to them speak for hours, I so enjoy their accents which seem to be a mixture of British and their indigenous language; perfectly complimenting each other, such a sophisticated mash-up. There is also a pragmatic way to their speech: to the point, no place for slangs and words like, kinda or sort of.

    Once that meet and greet concludes we go out for lunch. I am not too sure of the food yet so I choose an American dish. I figure there will be enough time to gradually taste their food, so why get sick on the first day. We turn in early that night, jet lag kicking our butts along with the time difference – South Africa being seven hours ahead of the East coast. There is so much to process; plus, I need to meditate as well to sufficiently ground myself in my new environment so that I can take full advantage of this opportunity. I know how I tend to live in my head so I decided before getting on the plane to enjoy every minute. Usually, once I become emotionally overwhelmed I retreat into my head and stay there until I feel safe; but the world doesn't wait for people to get over their issues, so I have missed many opportunities by chilling there, sometimes I miss whole conversations. This is going to be the most memorable trip for me ever so I am definitely going to be present for each and every moment. I just have to be really vigilant and not allow myself to be inundated by other people's emotions, which is going to be a huge challenge, having spent most of my life in my head but I am going to do it. It is going to be exhausting but I am going to rise to this challenge. Humans don't just unlearn years of conditioning over night but it is embedded in the human spirit to win and this I will.

    My folding days are over!

Chapter 10
The Meeting

Nathan

Auntie Toishma explained my sudden *uhanahaniso* (infatuation) even though it feels deeper than that but because it lacks merit I don't know what else to call it. I am still musing on her theory, not quite certain I'll be able to articulate much of what she said, but that's fine, who would I tell? No one would believe it anyways. I took her back to our village, because I don't know when next I'll be able to visit seeing that the American delegation is here. Unfortunately, I was unable to pick them up because of the heavy rain and I had to spend the night in my village. I feel badly about that but it just couldn't be helped. Also, it turns out that I am the third member of their team so I am team member and translator (because like most South Africans, I am a polyglot) and tour guide.

Currently, on my way to meet them but just my luck, of all the Freeways, I choose to take The Concrete Bypass also known as the N1, the busiest this time of the day. I am afraid that I am already making a bad impression on our visitors. They must think that I am quite unprofessional or I just do not take my job seriously.

In due course, I get to their hotel and as I get to the lobby, I can see that they are already waiting for me. I pause briefly to catch my breath and assess them from a distance. They both seem like keeners, they sport beautiful natural hair, pulled back in a tight bun at the nape of their neck. One is wearing far too much make up while the other one looks a little plain; however, she has her back turned to me so it's hard to tell. From all the way across the lobby, I can smell the sweet, fruity scent of their hair: the coconut oil being the most over powering and something else, maybe papaya. I guess no one informed them about the wide variety of wild life that will be attracted to their hair care products and I guess skincare products as well.

After a quick appraisal, I approach briskly in a business-like fashion. Instantly, I am hit with a sense of déjà vu, because I have lived this moment before. Here, right in front of these very eyes is my IG crush, the woman who has destabilized my very controlled environment. The one who has inserted herself into my every waking moment from the instant I clicked on her solitary image; my Shan squared. Just as I have found a way to rationalize my obsession, here she is in my very presence. My heart is racing as my pulse quickens, without a doubt I know that my palm is clammy and my face red.

Eagerly, I extend my hand by way of greeting but Shan Shan just stands there, gaping at me with a really queer look on her face. I guess she is very angry that I was unable to pick them up at the airport; so much so, that she is refusing to speak with me. Well, whatever words she lacks, her colleague has in an abundance.

She almost yells, "I am Kacia Peters and this is my team mate Shaney Phillpotts".

Kacia makes no attempt to hide her contempt. I file their names away: KP and SP.

"I don't know how things work around here, in Africa, but where we come from time is money and that is why we have been able to run very efficient systems over the years. We have been waiting here for the past hour. An hour that we will never get back. An hour that could have been better spent doing far more productive work".

She pauses to catch her breath then continues, her tone never changing from condescension.

"Is this really how you people treat important visitors to your country?"

I make no attempt to engage her or explain myself because; clearly, she has already made up her mind about South Africa and South Africans. She sees us as primitive; hence, inferior so my words would be wasted.

After a prolonged pause, which I took to mean that she has said what she intended, I offer a general apology without giving away too much specifics. At this point, I do not know how sincere it is but one thing is crystal clear; while Shan is the strong silent type, this one is the exact opposite and I can tell that this one is going to be a real peach to work with. Oh joy!

Shaney

It turns out that Glow and I have a few things in common. For instance, we are both workaholics, we value being on time and we like to get up early; which is exactly why my mom always says, it is impolite to judge. It is impolite because it leads to assumptions which then translate into stereotypes, evoking an emotional response and then we treat people accordingly. Today we've been up since the crack of dawn to get breakfast, prep for the day and take in the view. This view never gets old. The local guide is going to take us around after our meeting this afternoon. I'm a little disappointed that I won't have the solitude to go where I please. I guess that's life, you can not have it all. So, we're in the lobby, waiting and waiting for the guide; this guy has a real commitment problem or is it a time management problem?

Glow thinks it is "asymptomatic of the mindset of the people on this continent". Yes! Those were her exact words. I think she means symptomatic, but who cares! The real issue is, why did she even come on this trip if this is how she really feels about the souls on this continent? She definitely should have stayed home as this is clearly indicative of her mindset. I told you about her flamboyance which extends to her diction. This is really going to be a long trip. Sometimes, I wish I could just ditch her, just leave her and go wandering through the village like Mary Poppins. I just have a delirious desire to roam freely, to unfetter myself from all my insecurities. Pretty sure, Ms. Thing would think I have gone bunkers and she won't be going; after all, what if she meets Ebola. She actually said it, her exact words were:

"Girl, I'm not here to meet Ebola!"

I had to laugh out loud.

She added, "I'm just here for the warm weather - which is great for my hair and skin – and get the promotion that will come from this mission! I'm not about this kinda village life!"

I rolled on the floor laughing. She looked at me like I was Ebola.

We were told to meet our guide in the lobby at 2pm so we were there by 1:45. I had my back turned to the main door, browsing the magazine wrack. After about an hour, Glow says,

"This must be him. He sure took his sweet time getting here! I am going to give him a piece of my mind!"

I turned to her to warn her to be kind, then he was right next to me, extending his beautiful hands, exclaiming in his rich deep voice, "*Sanibonani*".

Obviously, since we've been here, we've heard this greeting many times, but it has never been this all consuming because here, right in front of me, live and in living colour is my Lion King. He says something about, Nathan. I think he's Nathan but I can't be sure. My brain has shut down on me, I can only stare. I know there is a word that I need to say but it is not coming to me and even if it did, my voice doesn't seem to be working either; so, I just stare in amazement. Which is all one can do in a crisis.

Luan must think that I am a complete idiot. Luckily, Glow has not lost her voice and she is in deed giving him a piece of her mind so while his attention is turned to her, I check out his profile. Thank God my eyes still work. I thought he was a dark-skinned man, but he's not. I thought all South Africans were dark skin, but not him. He is caramel mocha, a light brown colour. In fact, we have the same skin tone. How is that possible? He has broad, strong shoulders, perfectly even, white teeth, dark brown eyes, now ablaze with an intensity that I've never seen in anyone before. He is really well groomed. In some ways, I would expect no less from my Lion but in other ways, he is not who I was expecting. He is too suave, too debonair, way too charming. Even with Glow yelling at him, he is still pleasant and present. Yes, that's the word and that's his aura, present. And by present, I mean the full gamut of what it means to be present; he personifies present. I should know, I am rarely ever present, so I am quickly able to identify present.

I feel like I have been rendered incapacitated. Gradually, I am able to pull myself together so that I can join the monologue. But I hear his voice again, then I am hit by another wave of sentimentality which threatens to overwhelm me: it takes great resolve and restraint, which I don't have, to stay in the moment. Because usually I just allow my mind to wonder free – almost everyday, I have an out of body experience. In that, I go away in my mind and leave my body on autopilot. But not today!

From I stepped off the plane, even before I got here, this whole space has been calling me out. Calling me out of my comfort zone, beckoning for me to advance into my destiny. I sense that Luan's voice is the key which temporarily destabilizes me while simultaneously calls me back to my place on the planet, to my space, to my purpose in life. It's like a call from the ancestors, because yes, I am my ancestors' wildest dreams.

Finally, and slowly, I manage to address him and he takes my hand ever so gently and states, "Welcome to South Africa!"

With those words, spoken everyday by many and various people, that feeling of being home is complete. Now don't get me wrong, I am not describing a love at first sight encounter – although I foolishly thought it was – this is far more profound. It is a direct response to a yearning or hunger of the soul. I feel my face go red; this moment has got to be the most bizarre, atypical, mystifying encounter I have ever had. But true to my promise – I fight to stay in the moment – I will have to wait until later to sift through these impassioned stirrings. Right now, he wants to know what's on the agenda for today. I tell him and we are on our way – apparently Glow has said all she is going to say today. Fine by me, that girl is beyond rude. I will have to address her later about her contemptuous behaviour towards Luan. I am generally not confrontational but that was just not cool and totally uncalled for.

As it turns out, he is not just a regular tour guide but he is a member of the company that we are partnering with so he is able to address issues that pertain to the job and those that relate to the community at large. Also, now I don't have to spend all my free time on IG, because IG has come to me. Definitely, a win and a win.

Chapter 11

Kacia

For the life of me, I do not know what is wrong with Shan today. I have never seen her act this way before. I don't even know what to call her actions. All afternoon, she was looking at Nathan as if she wanted to devour him, as if he was both the entree and the dessert. The whole time, I just wanted to shake her and say, GIRL, GET A GRIP! Plus, I don't care how cute he is, or how charming, there is no way I am going to let him forget what he has done, the utter disregard he has shown for us and our time. I have learned that I shouldn't take disrespect from anyone and the first sign of rudeness should be dealt with expeditiously.

Obviously, I am going to have to be the one to keep him in check, I can not depend on Shan in this regard because she is already all doe eyed like Bambi. At first, she was quiet – which she generally is – but then she wouldn't shut up. I just spent the whole afternoon rolling my eyes. I am here to be efficient, do a fantastic job, think outside the box, explore new territories, blow everyone away, go home and get a promotion. Unlike Shan, I am certainly not here for the scenery; if I need scenery I will go to the Caribbean or Mexico. I am not here to just have a look see, neither I'm I here just to be cute either; cute is played out and it is infinitely overrated.

People just see me as the cute Black girl but what many have not yet recognised in me is my strong work ethic, that I am all about hard work. I work exceptionally hard because that is the only space from which

I derive my self worth, and this is one thing that I will not apologize for. I've always been the pretty Black girl or the girl who is pretty for a Black girl. Often times, I even feel unworthy of my job - the imposter syndrome – sometimes I think I am going to wake up, get dressed, go to work only to be laughed at and escorted out of the building. Most times, I seem so effervescent and it is to hide the fear and disguise the fact that I don't feel like I fit in. I envy Shan because she doesn't even care to fit in, half the fucking time, she is in LaLa land, she is not even paying attention. She doesn't give a shit about anyone or anything; yet here we are.

I also feel undeserving of love. I guess that too is tied to my sense of self worth which means that I always give too much of myself way too soon and then I have to maintain it so I always give too much; too much of myself, too much of my time. The last guy I dated was never on time, he forgot important milestones, and cheated constantly. That seems to be the story of my life: I definitely know how to skilfully pick winners. Therefore, I get really angry when people don't respect my time and my presence because I always feel like it is because I am insignificant why people would treat me like that. Well, no more of that crap. This little heart of mine is closed indefinitely for much needed repairs.

Naturally, with Nathan being so, so, so, handsome and so charming, I am not taking any chances – damn why did he have to be so damn handsome. Why couldn't he have looked like Kunta Kinte, I was actually prepared for Kunta, but here we are Mr. South Africa himself; fuck! Who knew they made men like him in Africa! Who knew! I am definitely going to have to maintain an acrid demeanour right up until I leave because every time I play nice, I lose and I am not about to lose, not this time.

I don't even want to know what is going on with Shan but she'd better figure it out soon and get her head in the game. I am not about to lose this contract and beyond my pleasant disposition is a tidal wave waiting to erupt.

Chapter 12

Nathan

 These two women could not be anymore different even if they tried. One is a little too inconsistent for me: one minute she is bubbly and vivacious and the next minute she is crass. Don't get me wrong, she is fiercely intelligent, that much is clear, you can see it in her eyes. She definitely has a wall up against me and I don't know why. But what she doesn't and would not know about me is that I am all about the pursuit. Call me morose, but I am traditional in the sense that I am all about the hunt. Plus, it is not in a woman's best interest to give too much too soon. There are a lot of takers out there and most women are naturally givers so they need to be extremely vigilant.

 On the other hand, Shan as Kacia calls her, is…what's the word…. *bedagsaam*, really thoughtful as in pensive. Seemingly, she is always in a dream and she has to fight really hard to stay awake. I guess that's what the Americans mean when they say "stay woke". She is really trying hard to stay woke. Nevertheless, I really like her. She has a childlike vibe – not childish – but pure and innocent. She even blushes sometimes, I have not seen a woman blush in a long time. I can't help but feel protective towards her; almost like a little sister or a cousin. As usual, aunt Toishma was right after all and I had no reason to stress about my feelings.

 Not withstanding, when it comes to Kacia, I'm not sure exactly how I feel about her. I am a bit frustrated, not with her, but with myself because usually I am so intuitive around people but with her I am completely locked out. Also, I see her stealing looks at me when she thinks I'm not looking. I am not too sure what to make of that. For instance, last week we had to visit a village, just outside Johannesburg and I had to translate from Xhosa to English for her, while she interviewed the locals or natives as she calls them. Clearly, she was impressed with my dexterity with language. But despite that, later when I tried talking to her she was back to her old cold self. She scurried behind her wall, like a scared chicken and closed all the curtains.

That being said, I am not looking for romance, but I am not opposed to it either. But by the same token, we are in a professional space so at the very least, she could be a little bit more collegial. Also, I am indeed grown enough to know when a woman is interested in me. I wonder who hurt her so badly that she has become a shell of herself.

Well, I guess she doesn't think I am worthy of her affection; after all, despite all my accomplishments in her eyes I am still just a boy from the Township or from the village, a bushman even. She probably thinks I have not yet earned my place in the world and I was probably just in the right place at the right time, to be apart of the right company. The more I think about it, why would she want little old me? When she is from America the Great, with a sense of entitlement and many options. I have had to work harder, laugh louder, be more than just ordinary to be seen as enough. People always look at me in a way that betrays their thoughts, like what did you have to do to get here? So why should Kacia be any different?

To be absolutely honest, I've never really fit in anywhere; not even in my family. Because, yes, we are Africans but I some how came out a little lighter in colour than the rest of my family members. So, they do love me but I am still viewed with a lot of cynicism, my motives always called into question, never quite trusted; loved but not in the way I need to be loved. Not withstanding, there is some amount of privilege that comes with me being the way I am, both in the villages and in Joburg (short for Johannesburg). I sometimes think that my job is proof of this. As a consequence, I have always fought for my place in the world and to find the right balance: the good with the bad, the ugliness of the world with all it's beauty.

Also, of necessity, I might have to abandon all hopes of even forming a friendship with Kacia which would be nice to stay in touch after all this is done; after all, "we are where we are" and que sera, que sera – "whatever will be, will be, the future is not ours to see". Some things just take more time than others maybe *poko-poko* (gradually) Kacia might come around. Well, they do have that braai this weekend. I really should just tell them *andizi* (I'm not going) and just see how Ms. Kacia reacts to that news. However, this is a less formal event so Kacia might just let her guard down. We will have to drive to Johannesburg, then fly to Cape Town and stay in a hotel, basically spend the weekend there. It is only four and a half hours in the air, not a long time but anything could happen when we land.

Shan is so much easier to deal with.

Chapter 13

Shaney

Before the barbecue or braai as Nathan calls it – I have really had to practise calling him Nathan so that I don't accidentally call him Lion again. I did once and to his credit he looked at me in that mischievous way of his and then we both burst out laughing, it was hilarious. But anyways, instead of heading straight to the event, we travelled to Western Cape, to visit Cape Town proper. Apparently, Western Cape is the province and Cape Town is like the capital city for that province. Nathan explained to us that just like Canada, they have Provinces (nine to be exact) which is the equivalent of the States in America.

Nathan said that Nelson Mandela had strong ties to Cape Town. His image has been immortalized in many statues and murals. It must be so inspiring to live in a city where the image of a Great Black man can be seen everywhere around you; instead of being bombarded by figures of the Confederacy. These overtly racist emblems by design; however triggering they maybe, tell a story of their own: they remind us not to forget our place in the world and how it was paid for in blood.

Cape Town is so naturally beautiful, as far as the eyes can see are stately mountain ranges, the most well known is Table Mountain. The land is flat in some areas, hilly in other parts, mostly rugged and undamaged, the prevailing colours are: greens, light browns and yellows – some of my favourite colours. Cape Town is magnificent, something out of a folktale, I wish we had stayed here instead but apparently safety might be an issue here. How could somewhere this beautiful present a threat to anyone? I look around and all I see is peace and tranquility.

Also, I really love the rich mix of modernity and indigenous artifacts which co-exist in Cape Town and its environs. By artifacts I mean, cottages and hut styled homes called Rondavel. Rondavels are oval shaped homes, with stone walls and a canopy made of luxurious dried grass and each is uniquely decorated: with various artwork and each door has a different colour. These homes are so colourful, they look like the off springs of the rainbow. I never had the pleasure of visiting one of these homes so I don't know what they look like on the inside but on the outside, they are very quaint. They are as diverse as the people who occupy them: some are quite stylishly made with bricks while others are understated. Hopefully, before we leave here, I'll be able to spend the night in one of these classic homes.

To complete the spectacular scene, there are numerous cascading waterfalls of differing sizes and variable force freely flowing over rocks in places that you would never imagine springs and waterfalls would be. I was so tempted to taste the crystal-clear water bubbling from the rocks like champagne but Glow kept insisting that I might get Ebola, so I decided against it. I thoroughly enjoyed driving in the countryside and let's face it, what's not to love: the fresh smell of soil after the rain and the flora the fauna are forever etched in my memory. After being in South Africa for a month, I am starting to wonder how I am ever going to adjust to life in New York after this.

On top of all that distinctive charm and magnetism there are many accessible and coastal beaches. Nathan promised to take us to the beach, I just hope he makes good on his promise before it is time to go and definitely not when I have my period. For one, the nuisance of it all and the frustration I would face in having to tell him.

Since we are already here for the weekend, we decided to make a trip of it; after all, when next will we be able to visit. We hiked up Table Mountain (so exhilarating and the view was to die for), visited Robben Island and the Two Oceans Aquarium. We even managed to get some wine tasting in. So much adventure, tucked away in paradise. By the time we got back to Pretoria, we were exhausted but it was worth it.

Chapter 14

Kacia

The barbecue was amazing, now these are my kind of people; they really know how to have fun. Our hosts served hamburgers, sausage and the most glorious kebabs I have ever eaten. However, they served something called *pap* which is some type of porridge, which I found utterly disgusting but Ms. Shan could not get enough of that horrible substance. Surprisingly, for the first time since I've met her, Shan seems to be in her element; Nathan seems impressed with her new zest for life. Also, they served something called a *braaibroodjie*, quite similar to a subway sandwich except there is no meat in the sandwich itself, it is eaten with the barbecued meat. Undoubtedly, there was wonderful, amazing, thrilling alcohol involved. I can not remember the last time I've had so much, good, clean fun or allowed myself to over indulge.

Plus, the natives are all so friendly; not at all as primitive as I thought they would be. As a matter of fact, I have come to learn that most of them are polyglots but they mostly speak very good English with a strong British undertone. I even complimented a few of the guests, "Your accent is lovely. Where did you learn to speak English so well?" They were quite polite but they looked at me kinda weird.

Later, when Nathan pulled me aside and explained that South Africa had been colonized by the British I understood the looks. He said that colonization started in 1652 by the Dutch, later the British took over and then there was ongoing oscillating rule between the two countries. In fact, Nathan said that colonialism and occupation only ended in 1961 which in the grand scheme of things is not that long ago.

He spoke to me like an equal, without condescension or any fanfare. Clearly, if ignorance was a crime then embarrassment must be my punishment. How am I so unaware of these things? In actuality, from the time I knew about this trip I should have studied their rich history. They know so much about America: from our news, politics, sports stars, entertainers, movie stars, to our history – the Middle Passage, slavery and the abolition of slavery. Why wouldn't they? Since I have been here I see how inundated they are with American culture and lifestyle. Compared to them, I feel like such an ignoramus even about some aspects of my own country. Nathan and his friends discuss International Politics and American politics as if they are all professors. They must think I am a complete imbecile.

I am forever indebted to Nathan for this kindness, for his tact in not calling me out publicly. Nathan is always kind and gentle. I could literally kick myself. How can I recover from this mistake? Here I am judging the natives, Nathan and Shan; especially Shan, when she clearly exercised due diligence. Imagine that, she is the one who almost always seems to be lost in translation, present but absent, but obviously here she is holding her own – being attentive to details. Meanwhile, Ms. Attention to Details has missed some of the fundamentals of this assignment. How am I going to sell a product that I know nothing about? Which begs the question, what else in my life have I been absent or excluded from as a result of my wilful ignorance? If Nathan had been a different person, this blunder could have easily cost me my job – not to mention the promotion that I so desperately need.

I really have to start doing and thinking about things differently starting from now; talk about an epiphany. Now I am starting to reflect on so many aspects of my life. How many opportunities have I missed? How many fruitful relationships have I rejected because I am too superficial in my perception? It is now as crystal clear as the spring water that Shan wanted to drink earlier, why I have been so vulnerable to love bombing by gas lighters. In retrospect, over the years, I have both misconstrued my significance in some people's life; while, diminishing my relevance to others. In that, I have come to reduce aspects of myself so that I could fit into other people's narratives, minimize my worth to make them want me.

No more of that crap, new day, new me. From now on, take all of me or just leave all of me, sir. Also, I have to get more hands on; in terms, of observing the culture and norms of refreshingly beautiful South Africa.

People say that we all experience an awakening at least once in our lives, who knew that mine would be here and now?

Chapter 15

Shaney

The barbecue or braai, as they call it, was so awesome: the food, the people, the conversation, the wine and so much of it, everything was perfect! I especially enjoyed the conversations, no small talk, solid discussions about a variety of interesting topics. As a matter of fact, when there was a natural lull in the exchange, there was no anxious gestures, everyone respectfully accepted the silence. Glow seemed to have had an amazing time, I have never seen her eat so much. She actually let her hair down today both literally and metaphorically. I even saw both her and Nathan in what seemed like a very intimate conversation. I felt a little jealous but oh well. He'll always be my Lion.

I met so many interesting, intelligent people with incredible life stories. For instance, there was an outrageously handsome Black man with scars on his face. When I enquired, Nathan explained that, "He is a Yoruba man and those are tribal marks" – mostly used for identification purposes". I've never seen anyone with scars like that before, a bit unnerving but striking nonetheless. I caught myself staring at him many times. He seemed to not mind at all. He seemed quite content in his own skin.

After that encounter, I started to reflect on a few things. One of them being my house mate and it came to me forcefully that Kacia's elaborate flamboyance is literally two-fold: on one level it represents her scars from past trauma; secondly, her superficial method of concealment. Ironically, that young man's scars are beautiful and unique;

also, I am quite sure there is a story behind his and his clan's choice in selecting each model for the scar, each tells a different narrative. We all have a story to tell, scars undeniably tell a multiplicity of stories and are the hallmark of a vanquisher. I have always believed that scars represent the real MVPs of the world, as they are the very epitome of survival.

I asked Nathan if he would ever get tribal marks. He said, "I am not sure. It is not mandatory for every clan so it is not something that I have really thought about". I guess in a sense, these markings are like tattoos, some people like them and others don't. It was my first time seeing any kind of tribal marks on a person and I must say that that young man's aura was so peaceful and calm, no signs of bitterness or remorse. There is such a quiet dignity in acceptance; certainly, an old word that I am learning new ways to embrace.

Nathan has promised to take us to his village this weekend – Graskop – that's what it is called. It even has a nice ring to it. Needless to say, I am so psyched – heck – even Kacia seems excited. As a matter of fact, she has not been herself since we went to the braai the last time; maybe, she is just starting to feel at home, just like me or maybe she is just coming into herself; again, just like me. She seems to have had a complete attitude change: no more walking around with her nose up in the air, sauntering around like a debutante at Homecoming or a princess. She is genuinely a sweet girl under all those many filters. Come to think of it, she doesn't even wear that much make up anymore. I am really happy for all these positive changes because before she was like a series of overlays on a Snapchat Filter, you never knew which version of her you would get on any given day. I guess under all that veneer of exuberance she is really just a scared little girl; much like the rest of us. Everyone is scarred in different ways – some are just more visible than others and some are better able to hide fears and scars.

I am learning more and more each day that Nathan is so easy to talk with, just as I had imagined. We even got around to discussing spirituality – which is something I almost never feel comfortable talking about. He shared that he is a follower of Taoism not really like hardcore but their ideology resonates with him. I have heard that term before but I never quite paid attention to it. Anyways, Nathan explained, "Taoism presents an acceptance of life as it is meant to be lived. No pretenses, no filters!" At that comment I looked at Glow who seems to have missed the reference.

Anyways, he went on to postulate that, "Just a sincere desire to become one with the natural rhythm of life. Thereby, accepting life with all its twists and turns, the good and the bad, all it's nuances". This seems rather fatalistic to me – which it might be – but such a charming notion. It rings like old school seduction. Kacia voiced what I was thinking, "That might prove too fatal for me". We all laughed but then she said, "Guys, I am serious though! What if you are heading towards a cliff and about to plummet to your death just because it happens to be 'the natural rhythm of your life' at the time". She does make a solid argument.

Nathan was quick to point out that, "Humans naturally have an innate desire to survive; therefore, despite this principle, the will to live is far more overpowering and strong enough to discern and avoid danger". I chimed in, "Taoism seems to highlight the principle of living in the moment". We all agreed that living in the moment is such an underrated and an unvalued experience in today's fast paced world. It has almost become a skill to be able to navigate the present and not rush ahead to the future or run back to the past; especially in times of great hardships and discomfort.

My lion is truly very smart, insightful and very sincere. He could literally be my twin. After that brief but intense discussion a noticeable weight seems to have lifted from our trio. Things are way less strained and more spontaneous. I even caught Kacia looking at my prince in a curious way, which is fine because they are kinda matched in terms of looks and brilliance.

Chapter 16

Kacia

"*Perhaps you're a slave to your own idea of yourself.*" D. H. Lawrence

It is not true what they say you know, that you can't miss what you never had because really you can. All these years, I have never allowed myself to have a true friend, not a male friend – heck - not even a female friend. As soon as I meet a guy, or see him on the street or on the Internet, I start planning our wedding. Therefore, I do not give myself a chance to date, to learn about the man before I fall and usually I fall pretty hard; heart first, never the head, oh no the brain is placed on pause. I strictly date to prep for my engagement and the wedding; not even fully taking into consideration, life after the wedding. Naturally, after a while when I hint at marriage and he would seem shocked and utter the words, *I like you but I am neither ready for a relationship nor marriage.* I would be genuinely shocked and heartbroken because I did not allow myself to observe or even see any of that. I would hear and see what I wanted to; regardless. A great way to break your own heart which I have done on many occasions.

But here we are in South Africa of all the places; among some of the most impoverished but I have actually started to see much more clearly than I have ever seen in my whole life. People who might not have all the luxuries of this life but they know contentment and they know how to love and laugh, not the fake laugh of the bourgeoise but a big, loud belly laugh. The simplicity of their way is compelling and their laughter infectious. Mind you, there are those who are filthy rich and make our celebrities look like paupers but the way of the common folk is so basic. I almost envy their lack of airs and pretenses; keeping up appearance for the Joneses, who don't even care is exhausting.

It is like the scales have fallen from my eyes and I am now experiencing a new birth, among people with strange customs that I would have never even considered before. They have accurately defined for me what true living is. Since I've been here, my sleep is restful, I walk slower observing the scenery and I listen, I actually hear what people have to say, instead of just hearing what I want to hear.

Essentially, all these years, I have been a squatter in my own life; almost someone akin to a door keeper, as I have just allowed all and sundry to roam freely in my sphere of existence without setting appropriate boundaries. That's the other thing, how I have seen South Africans live – how they devour every measly morsel of life. They live in the moment, unapologetically. I must admit that I have been stuck in survival mode from as far back as I can remember. Well really, why wouldn't they luxuriate in every moment of autonomy available to them – after being emancipated from the rigid structures entrenched in the system of Apartheid. But why wouldn't I, as well, seeing that I am the product of slaves? In such a short time, I have met many people from various clans, tribes, villages, towns, cities who all manifest such an unquenchable zest for life. They laugh like they have never cried, they saunter through life with determined strides as if they have never known strife or ever been embraced by the strong arm of oppression. In some villages, people live in huts, with little to no personal belongings, not much by way of accoutrements or luxury but they seem to have found the very essence of life – the very sustenance of the soul.

Meanwhile, I personally have been living like I am still enslaved, still in bonds. I have allowed myself to be a slave to my own perceptions and idiosyncrasies. Therefore, I have not truly learned how to just be me. Both Apartheid and slavery are merely disreputable generals from the same army who tried to break the indomitable spirit of the Black race. South Africans; however, have proven that their bodies might have been shackled but not their souls. Obviously, their vitality has not ebbed over the years. Nevertheless, here I am the descendant of former slaves – people who championed the cause of freedom, who vehemently opposed, even unto death, the ravages of the oppressor. A people whose deliberate crusades effected lasting change yet here I am held captive by my own limitations, my own imagination. All the time forgetting that, "I am my ancestors' wildest dream" as Shan keeps reminding us.

The fact that I am here on this continent – the very fact that my presence here is a rebellion against the desires of the oppressors who thought physically repositioning my ancestors would have erased them – would have obliterated their relatedness to the land of their birth – yet here I am. The very embodiment – the incarnation of a dream believed to be long dead. But in my physical presence, I have returned my ancestors home; after all, they were here before. I must therefore resist the compulsion to sink into the quagmire of despair and rise to the occasion to live my wildest dreams while being authentically me. To steel myself against disillusionment and forge a head with grace. After all, this is exactly what my ancestors, my people would have wanted.

Ultimately, I am very privileged to be here and it is also my right to be here – a right already paid for in blood. Some even gave their lives willingly so there's no way I am going to mess this up by living below my privileges. Plus, instead of trying to predict the future or orchestrate future events, I am just going to flow with the natural rhythm of life. I am no longer forcing anything because what is to be will be.

Chapter 17

Nathan

I pick up the girls from their hotel early in the morning to commence the four-and-a-half-hour journey to Graskop which invariably will take longer because there is so much to see, so much to embrace in this space. Once again, I muse at how much their hair smell like flowers, this must be the source of their #blackgirlmagic. On top of that, they are both wearing very floral rompers; a bit impractical for the journey ahead. How will they pee? And for sure a swarm of bees will most definitely find us at every turn as they both look like a forest barfed all over them. Undoubtedly, this is surely going to be a very intriguing trip.

It is a pleasant day – not too hot, not too humid, not too windy – just absolutely perfect. The girls say it is the best weather condition for their hair. We drive with the windows down. Although I have lived here for almost all my life, and have experienced it so many times, this place and its magic, never gets old. It is an age-old magic, sometimes heard echoing in the wind, left behind to remind us of the strength of our ancestors. How can one ever behold and hold perfection then get use to it? Do we ever get use to staring at the Mona Lisa? No, never!

Shan and Kacia marvel at the pristine natural beauty and are quite anxious to experience the Panorama Route. They squeal in joy at the sight of birds and the small animals flourishing in their natural habitat. And of course, they have already taken about a hundred pictures between them and hoping aloud that Apple will not let them down and their batteries will last.

THEY WERE HERE BEFORE 57

Since their hotel is in Pretoria, we stop to tour the Union Buildings, Freedom Park, take pictures under the Jacaranda trees, which are burgeoning and are the very manifestation of majestic. Then we cruise through Long Tom Pass and get a panoramic view of the various falls. The ladies have gone quiet but their eyes and their vibrancy speak volumes. They are like two little kids in a candy store but instead of candy, they have iPhones.

Eventually, we stop for a picnic lunch. We eat in the car (we've already been attacked by bees twice) and take in the lush undisturbed vegetation. Before today, I doubt we could get Kacia to sit in a car and eat. Oh, how has the mighty fallen? I am awashed with memories from my childhood and unabashed pride at the natural beauty of my homeland. Picturesque being an understatement.

Everything is going well until later in the evening when we get to the Shangana Cultural Village. We get out the car to visit the many stalls buried under the most amazing crafts to be found in the country or even the world. Quite unexpectedly, both Shan and Kacia experience unmistakably visceral reactions as soon as we were in the confines of the village. It is the absolutely most astounding manifestation – for lack of a better word – I have ever been privy to in my life.

Shan

This trip, is unequivocally the most exhilarating experience of my life, from the trees, to the small springs, the mountain range in the distance, the clear blue sky, the birds, even the nuisance bees; everything is tantalizing to the senses.

All is well, until we enter the Shangana Cultural Village and my life is forever changed. I recognize vibe and energy more quickly than words and the vibe in this space is straight out of a Hollywood horror film. I feel an improbable connection to this place – it is literally as if I have been here before. The most profound thing happened; usually, when I have to do bloodwork, I can only give blood from my right arm because none of my other veins work, they are too tiny. The only vein which works is the Brachial Vein (that's what the nurses always say) so this is the only vein that is always visible and easily accessible. As soon as we drive into the compound, this very unique vein starts to pulsate vigorously. Meanwhile, the inner part of my elbow become blood red. I check to see if I had been stung by a strange bug or one of those bees which may have caused an allergic reaction but there is no indication that it is either of those things. The very ectoplasm of my bloodline comes to attention. Every hair on my head is on full alert. My life has come full circle and I am undoubtedly home. Nathan and Kacia come to my aid as they could see my distress. Although I might have the look of the bewildered but there is no discomfort just a serene sense of nostalgia.

When they gather around me, I feel invisible hands reach out and embrace me; ever so gently and stroke my hair. Even the slight breeze feels like a whisper from the ages, marked by a recognition and familiarity which tenderly says,

"Sanibonani! Welcome home child!"

Kacia

We are having such an absolutely marvellous time: the food, the company; even the occasional silence is germane to the theme of the day: harmony. Suddenly, I feel like I've been struck in the face which is followed by a strong gust of wind as a result of the impact of the blow. I scream in agony as more blows come; each more ferocious than the next. Nathan is speaking to me, I think he is asking if I am ok.

Soon the villagers start to congregate but their previously affable faces are drenched in bitter indignation. They start yelling at us, at me "PHUMA! PHUMA!" I don't know what they are saying but their words and expressions do not represent a welcome mat: between cowering behind my hands and trying to determine what they are saying I am awashed with fear and trepidation.

I try to get back in the car because these amiable people are now reaching for stones. Nathan, by far the strongest among us is frozen in blind horror, he looks like he is in a daze. It is Shan who jumps into action. She's screaming, "Get in the car! Get in the car!" I think I am screaming as well: a loud piercing sound which reverberates through my whole being. It is an ugly, primitive, guttural sound which comes from the deepest recesses of my being. I sound like a wounded animal; even in the moment I can not believe that this is me. This is what I have come to. This is somehow what I have been reduced to. I think for sure I am going to die. My shrill shrieks jerk Nathan back to the present. He immediately moves into action, pulling the car door, almost knocking me down, he grabs me, sweeps me off my feet and flings me in the back of the car and stuffs me in, like a sack of potatoes. He jumps in the passenger seat as Shan takes the wheel.

Objects are thrown at the car as we drive away but the pummelling to my body has stopped. I don't remember anything else because the world suddenly goes dark as if someone has abruptly turned off the lights indicating that the party is over. Before the lights go out, one thought hits me: is this where my story ends!

Chapter 18

Nathan

I am mesmerized by the scene as it unfolds in front of me; so much so, that my fight or flight instinct doesn't kick in right a way and I am paralyzed both literally and metaphorically. I stand there incapacitated for God knows how long! How could this calm and hospitable community just erupt into utter pandemonium. The Shangana people are renown for their peaceful ways – which is natural as they are surrounded by nature for miles and miles; therefore, they have become one with their surroundings. I wonder how did things suddenly escalate so quickly, from being worried about batteries dying to now worrying about Kacia's safety.

Come to think of it, I know that in the recent past there has been a spate of xenophobic attacks against foreigners; but not Americans – mostly migrants from the Continent. I am at a loss – why would they react to Kacia this way – because apparently, she was their target. Obviously, Kacia is an American – sure she looks like us – but there are tell tale signs in her mannerism and aura of entitlement. If in nothing else, her mode of dressing is conspicuous in this intentionally antiquated habitat. How could something like this happen? It was my job to protect them. I had one job but instead I brought them into the den of lions.

Shan

I have often heard people talk about a defining moment. This place in time will forever be mine. While I stood there being embraced by invisible forces with such a deep awareness of harmony, it seemed like I stepped out of my body for a minute. I was transported to a scene where there were literally thousands of people: working, talking, just an overpowering sense of community. In fact, some of them look exactly like me and my family members; and although, no words were spoken – well that's not accurate – none that I could grasp the usual way. Their words seem to flow over me and flow through me. Also, there is a distinctive quality in how they address each other – a kind of authentic reverence. I watch as this quality vanishes in the wind, as in the same field of vision: the goodwill is broken by strange visitors (in my mind I discern that they are slave traders) but in the people's perception, they are just visitors. That's the other piece to this vision, I perceive instinctively what and how they see. Someone comes close and touches me and as I turn and look in her face, into her brilliant eyes; immediately, I know that she is a significant part of me: an aunt, no a great, great, great, great, great grandmother. She looks exactly like me except older – but she wears absolutely no wrinkles and there in that smile, my mother's smile.

However, despite the beauty of the moment there is an immeasurable sadness, a great longing for things long lost or stolen. So many things have been lost or stolen. I want to cry a million tears for her, for their way, for my ancestors who have returned to let me know that they were here before. And I now know for sure that because they were, I am and I have a right to be here. That has got to be the most liberating piece of knowledge that can be transmitted from one generation to the next. In that moment, I vow to own my place in the world and not shrink to accommodate bigots, imperialism and other such ideologies entrenched in racism, to keep me and others like me out of our rightful place.

Suddenly, she is saying something very hurriedly, but I can no longer comprehend what she is saying, there is now a look of terror in her eyes and a new urgency in her actions. Vigorously, she is pushing me – pushing me away with every ounce of energy that she has to spare and she is exclaiming,

"Phuma!"

There is an abrasive sound, like an explosion and immediately I am back in the present and someone screams – a gut wrenching cry – and a word erupts from me RUN! I quickly examine the angry scene but who are they angry with and why? With great horror, I realize that it is Kacia. She is hunkering down with hands raised across her face in a protective stance screaming bloody murder, in a way I have never seen her before. I think, those skinny arms will not protect her, not now, not ever.

I am terrified and fear pushes me into action. I grab the keys from Nathan's pocket because he too is in a trancelike state and rendered motionless as if riveted to the spot. I shake him while simultaneously trying to get the driver's door open. Every fiber of my being is hollering, LEAVE! SAVE YOURSELF! SHE'S NOT WORTHY! I don't know where that comes from but intuitively I know that I can not leave my friends. I am halfway in the car, one hand pressing hard on the horn while simultaneously reaching up to slap Nathan in the face. Instantly, he comes alive - like I have activated him - and not a moment too soon as the mob is occupying too much of our personal space. Everything happens in high definition, slow motion, he grabs Kacia, throws her in the backseat, tucks her in and jumps in the passenger seat next to me.

I really don't want to harm anyone but it is either them or us and my survival instincts have kicked into high gear. I reverse a little, horn blaring and then I accelerate, away from the unsettling crowd that is getting thicker by the minute. Where did so many people come from all of a sudden? I am pretty sure, there were not that many people milling around when we first got here. We drive for about thirty minutes and once we clear the village we stop to check on Kacia. She is breathing but just barely. She is going into shock. Shock is a paradox as it is both beneficial and destructive to the human body. It provides a respite in times of crisis but can lead to a potentially dangerous outcome; for instance, a cardiac arrest. I pray silently that this is not the case.

I yell at Nathan, "We need to take her to a hospital!"

He says, "No! There's not enough time! It's too far!"

"What are we going to do then?" I scream. "We can't just keep her here. What if she had a heart attack or suffered internal bleeding?"

Apparently, he arrives at a decision that he is certain of.

"We have to take her to my village. My aunt Toishma will take care of her".

Silently and vehemently I pray that she can be trusted and she won't turn savage on us like the Shangana people.

With his new-found certainty, he confidently takes the steering wheel as I move to the back to offer whatever comfort I can to Kacia, keeping her face moist, with ice from our picnic. How could such a beautiful day, take such an ugly turn! I look out the window as the rain approaches from the west. I smell the rich, earthy aroma before I see the first drop. I close my eyes as the raindrops hit the car angrily. Even the weather has turned against us.

Chapter 19

Nathan

The heavy rain slows us down considerably but we make it to aunt Toishma without much incident. The rain has always had a very calming effect on me; but not today.

Kacia is fitfully asleep in aunt Toishma's bed. There is sporadic fighting and screaming while she sleeps which is so painful to watch; much like watching a car collide with a bear, feeling too frail to assist. I wish I could help her but how am I going to fight an invisible adversary? That sense of being powerless, has got to be the single most debilitating feeling in the world.

She revived late in the night after auntie gave her an elixir of herbs, believed to be some of the most potent throughout Africa. She is bruised all over - even though we're not entirely sure how - because she wasn't hit that many times by the villagers. Thankfully, she's alive and where there's life, there is hope; everything else can be sorted out, at least that's what they say. I reflect on all the clichés about hope (how it springs eternal in the human breast, etc.) and not a single one is compelling enough to ease my troubled mind.

By necessity, we have to spend the rest of the weekend here until Kacia gets her strength back. We could actually drive back early Monday morning for work which would give her two full days to recover since today is Friday.

I can already tell that it is going to be a long night. I am still bewildered about what happened in the village. Shan who is generally quiet seems to have slipped far away into herself. She seems far removed from the present. I have to keep guard over both of them. Earlier Shan told me what had happened, about her vein being quite pronounced and pulsating, I actually saw it moving, before the attack on Kacia. I am way too floored to process what has transpired and what is still trending. My aunt promises to explain things to us once Kacia is stronger. This I really have to hear, there is absolutely no explanation for all this. It is one of those misnomers that is too far fetched and too far removed from the realm of human comprehension to be considered real. Never in my wildest dreams could I or would I have predicted the day's events.

To the Americans we must seem so ratchet and savage and how could anyone blame them! But the truth is, this is not our way. We are a warm and hospitable people even the very poor among us is the most hospitable of all of us; that is our way. This open hostility towards a poor defenseless girl is atypical of Africans; especially the Shangana people. I really hope she will accept my apology and forgive my people for their error in judgment. They must have mistaken her for someone else. But who?

Shan

I have always felt that all human beings come with a wealth of experiences and all the experiences are stored in a museum somewhere that we all can call up at will; almost like a panoramic view like we passed earlier. Therefore, we are beholden to humanity to share our experiences to contribute to this bank of lived experience so that history does not repeat itself.

However, I am still processing everything that has happened today. I will never be able to divulge all the things that happened in my dreamlike state. How would I be able to explain that to rational people? They are bound to think that I am crazy or worse that I am on drugs. As much as Nathan is a very perceptive person, this would not bode well with him. There is no way in hell I am ever telling anyone about that episode.

Plus, it was such a profoundly beautiful and personal encounter that I am not even ready to share it or even have the words to share it. How many people get a chance to go back in time and meet their ancestors? This story is all mine now but once I share it, it belongs to someone else to do with it what they please. It will become apart of their experience portfolio because even vicarious experiences contribute to making us who we are and impact how we evolve or devolve as humans.

Kacia

I feel bruised all over and I am in excruciating pain from the crown of my head to the sole of my feet. I am in a house that I don't even recognize. I feel exhausted and my head is spinning. I think I have been sleeping for a whole day and I don't even know what day it is. Nathan has fallen asleep in the chair next to my bed – well someone's bed. He looks horrible, poor guy! I am terrified to go back to sleep because all those invisible hands grabbing at me today, slapping me, have all appeared in my dream and they all have faces – horrible faces. Not horrible as in ugly but horrible as in hateful. Their faces are distorted with rage and bitterness. What have I ever done to inherit all of this? Why do they hate me so much; so much so, that they haunt me continuously in my dreams? I surmise that this is not just a dreamlike state; their rage though misplaced is too heartfelt not to be real. The rage is too authentic, too intrinsic to be fake.

What have I gotten myself into this time? I feel the heavy grip of sleep pulling me back into a world that I must flee but like a small fish being pulled from the ocean resistance is futile. It is useless to resist the overwhelming tug of sleep, I give up. I can't fight anymore. I have no more strength left. Ironically, I am surrounded by people who genuinely care; yet I must fight alone. I guess this is where I die. My poor mother, for sure she will die too. How will they explain cause of death to her? I have made it my responsibility to eat healthy avoiding carbohydrates as much as possible, stay hydrated, exercise when I can, practise yoga and being kind, moisturize, mind my own business; now look at me! If I live through this, I'm going to try every single ice cream flavour there is and that's a promise!

Chapter 20

Nathan

I try to ward off sleep for as long as I can, like when I was just a boy and I wanted to stay up late with my older cousins to hear stories about *Anansi*, the trickster figure, whose ingenuity always wins in the end. However, it is as if, I have had *Wild Dagga*, a plant well-known for its sleep-inducing property; I am way too exhausted to fight anymore. You know how sometimes, you gently sink into a peaceful sleep and slowly become aware of a dream; not me, not tonight. I am immediately plunged into a very harsh dream; Kacia and Shan are there as well. Once again, Kacia is under attack. I rush in, guns a blazed as the Americans would say, except there is no gun, ignoring the apparent danger to myself. I hear myself command, "*Yeka lokhu!*" Stop this! "*Lokhu akusikho njengabantu!*" This is not us, as a people! Why am I speaking Zulu, a language I hardly speak? Kacia's assailants immediately turn their attention to me like sunbathers facing Apollo.

At this point, I am operating purely on adrenaline and I can not even lie, I am scared beyond measure. I have never been this terrified in my whole life. It is not just the people and their strange clothing, or the sounds, or their grimacing and flailing, it is the place, it evokes a fear that is almost tangible; a fearful reverence. Intuitively, I know that this is a majestic place for the exalted, not a place for a weakling like me. Now that I have their attention, I fumble in my mind to find the most logical argument. As I am about to speak, something peculiar happens, as if on cue; they all bow their heads, an obeisance indicative of high honor. I am rendered speechless. Why are they doing this? Who are these people? Could they be my people? Instinctively, I know that I originated from them; that they were here before. But how are they here now? Why am I here now, in this place, at this time? What is the meaning of this?

Then after a silence that stretches for an eternity, so jarring, I feel it echo in my body, in my veins, like a delayed pulse; so much so, that I believe my heart would be silenced indefinitely: Shan takes charge of this extraordinary situation. Wonders never cease! Seemingly, she commands their attention like a true monarch. But as if that in itself is not confusing enough, what she says next sends shivers down my spine: "*Lalela inkosann yakho!*" Listen to your prince! Is Shan speaking Zulu? Why? How? What the *Mka* is going on here?

Immediately, I turn around - relief flooding me - to see this prince who has made an appearance, because I really would like to have a word with him. Plus, someone needs to take charge here and reveal to me (very slowly) what in the fuck is going on here. But alas, to my great and utter chagrin, no one is standing there; just me. Just me, in my mind I see myself clearly, a small boy, where a man should be. Is this how I have always seen myself – a mere effigy - of whom I am meant to be? Shan moves closer to me and instructs me like a trusted advisor, "Tell them to release the prisoner. I`ll explain everything later!"

I am light headed! Is this going to be my permanent state from now on; light headedness? Because that is all I have been feeling all afternoon; light headed. I have experienced all the symptoms of a full-blown panic attack; however, the most terrifying is still looming -hyperventilation. Despite that and maybe because of that; the significance of the moment is not lost on me, as I am suddenly and painfully aware that Kacia's life greatly depends on everything I do, say, my tone and even my body language from here on. With a quiver in my voice, which I am useless to conceal, I command my people – who else could they be – I command them to "*Muyeke ahambe*!" Let her go! This command is met with immediate and vehement protest. I am no prince and that much is clear. However, I still have to try, so I raise my hand in a resolute stance and I search deep within for a harsh reprimanding glare. I guess it works. They reluctantly release Kacia. She is shaking from exhaustion and fear. Shan rushes to soothe, her lips moving quietly.

Surprisingly, I am awake, alive but quite unwell and back in Toishma's hut again – my stomach doing flips, drenched in sweat. Thankfully, it wasn't any other bodily fluids. What in thunderation is going on here? I make a silent vow to myself, from now on, I am never going back to sleep, not today, not tomorrow, not next month, not ever.

Chapter 21

Nathan

    This has been the longest day and the most perplexing night of my life! I stay up for the rest of the night. I do everything in my power to stay awake because I do not want to return to that place; to that place of sacrifice. I now know for certain that it is much too dangerous for Kacia to remain here in Graskop and the surrounding areas. I have to take her back to Pretoria, she was much better there. There are bad spirits out to get her here. Maybe she has been bewitched? But why here? Why now? Why her? Why is her presence here so disruptive to the natural order of things? I have so many questions.

    Thankfully, auntie is an early riser and apparently so is Shan because she is wide eyed and bushy tail. I quickly tell them my dream - there is absolutely no way I am keeping all that horror locked away in myself – that would be detrimental to my overall emotional health. But for some reason none of them seems surprised or disturbed by this dream. Shan especially surprises me, she says, "I had the very same dream". Now, I have heard about a lot of weird shit in my life but dream sharing is definitely not one of them. Auntie, as efficient as a colony of ants says, "Let's have some breakfast and then we can talk about this. You kids didn't have dinner last night".

    Yes, let's talk about this because I'm about to lose my mind here so someone better have an explanation and not just any explanation but a plausible one. That being said, not for the first time in my life have (I am sure this will not be the last) I wondered about my aunt's sense of

THEY WERE HERE BEFORE

calm in the most tumultuous situations! Certainly, if this is not tumultuous, I don't know what is. However, her tranquility is both soothing and infectious. I feel panic falling back and I am grateful because now more than ever, I have to keep my wits about me. Above all else, I have a mandated responsibility both morally and professionally to take care of Shan and Kacia, I gave my word and my word is my bond. And who would I be, if I am unable to keep my word? Even with a growing sense of powerlessness, I still have to hold true to the very essence of my identity. Yes, I am Xhosa and nothing is going to ever change that. I come from strong people who have always embodied integrity and decency. That is a part of me that will never change neither would I want to change.

While Shan and I stare at our breakfast, occasionally sipping sweet tea, auntie attends to Kacia: bathing and dressing her wounds, feeding her, then drenching her with more herbs. Some of the most powerful natural remedies known to my people: *Rooibos, Buchu, Sour figs* and *Aloe Vera*; these botanicals have been used for centuries to cure everything from the common cold to more serious ailments. Older folks swear by them, to the point where, if they don't cure the sick, his family starts to plan his funeral.

When they finally make an appearance, Kacia looks surprisingly better than I expected under the circumstances. After we are all settled, aunt Toishma spins a tale so outrageous that it has to be true. Plus, I have never known my aunt to lie or trivialize a situation so it has to be her truth. Also, I remember many times when she has spoken peace and calm into existence in stressful situations. Mind you, this narrative does not bring peace or calm to anyone but as always auntie's sense of calm, from her voice to her posture, commands our attention and destabilizes fear.

Chapter 22
Aunt Toishma's Tale

"The past is never dead. It's not even past". William Faulkner

I have absolutely no desire to scare these children but I must to be honest with them.

I have to tell them truths about their ancestry. So many times, as parents, we think that we are protecting our children by keeping secrets from them or by telling them half truths; however, they can be just as easily hurt by what they don't know as much as what they do know. In fact, one of our enduring proverbs is: *One who bathes willingly in cold water doesn't feel the cold.* This simply means that once we face our fears we take away their power to hurt us.

I have always known that Nathan is special even as far back as when he was a child. He has always manifested a sobriety far beyond his years. Now that time and chance have brought these three together they have set off alarms in the spiritual realm. This is going to be a very difficult conversation.

"Nathan, do you remember the folklore about the Zulu prince wanting to marry the Shangana princess?"

"Yes auntie. But what does a myth, passed down through oral history have to do with the shenanigans of yesterday? Plus, we're not Zulu, we are Xhosa people are we not?"

"Nathan, it is more than just a tale, it is more than lore: it is truth and a part of our history. Originally, our ancestors were Zulu, some of our direct descendants even fought along side Shaka Zulu in the Zulu wars. However, over the years through the process of migration, intermarriage; among other extemporaneous circumstances, we became both Xhosa and Zulu. Eventually, we were completely disconnected from our Zulu heritage".

All three of them begin to speak simultaneously. I raise my hand for silence because what I have to tell them is far too important for interruption: I will only have enough time to say it just once and then they will have to leave.

"Children, I will tell you as much as I can! But you have to listen attentively without disruption and then you guys have to leave immediately. Is that clear everyone?"

They all look so frightened like children lost in the forest at night; especially, Nathan. A huge part of his identity, is being ripped away from him without any warning; that must be a tough pill to swallow. I really want to soothe them but there really is no time. I will fill in the gaps for Nathan at another time. Also, there is no easy or safe way to say this. I resume my narrative.

Some parts of the lore have been excluded over time; you know how it is with humans and their memory. In the absence of a system for writing we forget things, life is complex and at times complicated so we only keep things in our memory that are most immediate to our situation. Therefore, after the main players died, there was no one left to be custodians of our heritage so this tale has been misplaced and mistreated. Critical to an understanding of this tale is that the prince and the princess were truly in love. His love was never unrequited as the people were led to believe; they both suffered and died as a result of the love that they had lost. An important part of the narrative is that close relatives of the prince and the princess would return to their ancestral lands at the exact same time. They would get married in order to appease the spirit of the long dead prince; to give him peace so that he can finally rest. Thereby, fixing the past so that you can cement the future.

Nathan and Shan, you were immediately attracted to each other because you share the same ancestry, the same heritage, the same bloodline. I am now fully convinced especially because of the fact that you guys shared the same dream earlier. This further indicates that you guys are closely related genetically. Therefore, what you mistook for a *mangalisayo* or a romantic connection was actually, *igazi libiza igazi*, which loosely translates to blood calling out to or for blood. A deep calling for a bond that withstands the test of time, which is more like a soul connection. Shan, as soon as, Nathan saw you on his computer, or phone, or whatever you young people use to communicate and I am also sure that the feeling was mutual when you saw him as well; there was an immediate connection. At this conclusion, they both blush and look away.

The ancestors knew that it was time for the long-declared prophecy to be fulfilled. The three of you did not just happen to come together by chance or choice; this has been a pre-determined alliance. Shan, your eyes see what Nathan can't so that you can better advise him. Also, you have been granted the ability to see into the past so that you can help Nathan to correct the future, so that the same mistakes aren't made again.

As humans, we like to think we have complete autonomy over our life and we do to a great extent but there is also a huge part of our existence which has been predestined or ordained from birth. This is a difficult concept to embrace; especially, in Western cultures because children are raised to believe the exact opposite, that they alone control their destiny. This mode of thinking excludes our responsibility to our clan, tribe or community which leads to *ubugovu obukhulu* or great selfishness. Selfishness is a learned behaviour and was never the way of our people. But like a thief in the night, egotism and selfish ambition crept in which led to a disruption and the eventual destruction of the old ways.

The other issue is, in the West and to some extent even here in South Africa, people have come to believe that every time they feel attracted to someone that it is *uthando* or a romantic connection; but it is not always. It is sometimes a soul connection or *ukuxhumana komphefumlo*. A much deeper connection than a mere sexual attraction. I am not saying, that a sexual attraction is insignificant, as a woman who has been married twice, I would be remissed to be so limited in my thinking. However, there is stark contrast between a soul connection and a sexual one; my first marriage was based almost entirely on a sexual connection but this my second marriage is more balanced because it is both.

Kacia, obviously you are a direct descendant of the Shangana princess and for some reason, your ancestors have hand picked you to pay the penance, make atonement, or fulfill the mandate; it depends on how you want to look at it. However, our ancestors, the Zulus are still so angry that the only thing that will appease them now is your blood. Before, they would have been appeased if the princess had been returned to the prince; however, at this point in the game: it is blood for blood, *Igazi ngegazi*. The people who attacked you in the village are actually from the Zulu tribe.

At this point Shan interjects, "But aren't all Africans related? Why are there so much infightings, if they are all one people?"

"Great question Shan; however, the complexity between the Shangana and the Zulus and in deed all African nations, are way too nuanced to explain at this point; maybe, at another time when time isn't of the essence".

She doesn't seem satisfied, but it's the best answer I have, given what we are up against.

I continue, "They have some how sensed that you are directly related to the late princess. Some people are still in touch with the ancestors so they are allowed to sense things and sometimes they are propelled by the ancestors to act".

I pause after this declaration and take in each of their reaction. They all register great shock and disbelief but I have no time to offer solace because they have to leave and soon. Shaney questions, "So you mean, not every seemingly romantic attraction is of a romantic nature?"

I sigh, not to be rude but because I don't have time for this, but they do have a right to be heard and their concerns addressed.

"Yes, that's true. Over time, people move from place to place, from city to city from country to country. So gradually there is an intermixing of bloodlines. Plus, with our history of some of our people being taken, dragged to far afield places, there has been a blending of bloodlines; but the ancestors always know. Back in the day, everyone was aware of their tribe or clan, their unique place in the scheme of things, but with time this has changed and people who share ancestry: meet, fall in love, get married and have children. But really, it is a familial connection to a kinsman or kinswoman and not romantic love. Familial connections are so strong that they impact us in far more substantial ways than we think.

Also, the other thing which might spark a connection is a shared trauma. For instance, it was an extremely traumatic event for our people to be snatched from the land of their birth, the land that we have been so connected to for so many years. Naturally, this trauma has been passed on in our DNA so sometimes when people meet and feel an instant connection it is their deep-seated trauma that attracts them to each other. Again, this is not always the case but it is not always romance which is why so many of these, trauma induced relationships end up failing because that is no foundation on which to build a lasting relationship.

Kacia speaks for the first time, "That is so remarkable and makes perfect sense for me. Because sometimes I meet people who feel like home and smell like home – for a lack of a better word - those relationships have never ever worked for me". She continues, "I have always felt that my life was rigged somehow. I always seemed to pick the wrong relationships, or the right one at the wrong time, or sabotage the potentially right ones. But when I met Nathan, it felt different and the difference scared me. Nathan, I apologise for all the times when I was rude to you. I just wanted to push you away to protect myself."

Nathan says, "That's cool. Life happens sometimes and if what auntie says is true…"

"What do you mean, if it is true? Shan's turn to speak up. "What other possible explanation could there be? How else could we explain Kacia's attack and all the madness that has been going on?"

I must intervene here because while all these questions are valid we are running out of time. Time is of the essence. Kacia questions, "How are you so sure that I will ever be safe in Pretoria now that they have been alerted to my presence here?"

Nathan answers quickly, "It is not seen as their traditional Zulu land so the ancestors will not encroach on lands that they have never owned.

THEY WERE HERE BEFORE

They are very honourable and some boundaries they will never cross."

"It makes sense if you think about it! Up until yesterday, you were perfectly fine, right?" Shan theorizes.

They all seem to get the message at the same time. They all spring into action simultaneously: bumping into each other, grabbing stuff and hugging me alternately, saying good bye and hugging each other.

They leave right away yelling their thanks as they enter the car and not a moment too soon. It is now 5:30am, they should be in the clear. At around 6 am, there is suddenly a loud banging on the door. I open it but there is no one there. I wasn't expecting to see anyone. I know it is the ancestors who have come to extract Kacia. I am unafraid because they don't have any grouse with me plus I am not the prize; thankfully. They still operate on an honour principle, so no harm will come to me; that is just their way. So, for now, I am not sure but I think they will perhaps strategize, they might still pursue Kacia or find another person from another generation, the good thing is, there is always just one per generation or every third or fourth generation. I don't know for sure, no one knows for sure the ways of the ancestors; we can only rely on their sense of decency and loyalty to their off springs. For now, and for this reason, dear sweet Kacia will be safe. I don't know if both her and Nathan will marry; that's entirely up to them. The ancestors have not given me the *ihlo*, the eyes to see the future, I can only pray to God that everything will work out well for both of them.

Chapter 23

Kacia

"The past beats inside me like a second heart". John Banville

I know that I am being crazy and I sense that the others believe this to be the case, but what other choice do I have. Suddenly, I have a compulsion to do this and I feel that I must. I asked Nathan to drive back to the Shangana Craft Market, where all the mayhem unfolded, what seems like moments ago. He says, "Are you out of your God damn mind?" I said, "Possibly, but I absolutely have to do this". He says a little more gently, "You do know that once you are there, I can not protect you. I have no control over anything from that point onwards. What little power I have, is here, driving this car". I tell him that I understand and I am deeply touched by his great desire to protect me but I really feel like I have to do this.

Eventually, Shan says, "While I can not protect you, I sense when they are near. I know it's weird so please don't ask how". I said, "Ok". She goes on, "I will go with you and let you know when things are getting out of hand". Nathan says, "I'll go with you as well. I truly respect you for doing this although I still think you're crazy". We all laugh and walk tentatively to the entrance of the empty market; empty as far as we can see. But with a sigh, I sense that they are gathered there, waiting for me. Straightway, a calm I have never known washes over me and I know that I am doing the right thing. I know that somehow, I have been appointed to do this, to carry out this deed on behalf of the ancestors. I stand a few feet away from my friends because I would not want them to get hurt because of me and then in a language I have never spoken, I hear myself say:

I am so deeply sorry for all the trouble, all the hurt and pain caused by my people all those years ago. I wish I could go back and do things differently, make amends. But I can not just like how you can not change the past by disrupting the future. So please forgive the mistakes of my father, he was just really scared that he would lose me forever. He was a very proud man and would never admit fear but that is all it was a father's frantic fear. Also, I am sorry for all the innocent people who lost their lives and their loved ones and while I can not return them to their families, I can promise you that in my own life, I endeavoured to never inflict harm on anyone, as much as it was in my power. I died just like my love, a lone and heart broken. Shouldn't that count for something that we both died the same death, the death of the broken? I did not get the opportunity to mother children. How could I, they would never be his? Never marrying and therefore never fulfilling my dream to be a mother of great warriors. How could they be and he wouldn't been able to father them and train them?

At that Shan starts to beckon to me in a very aggressive manner, to get away from there. I quickly add in English, "If it is any consolation, the princess has suffered as well. She lost the love of her life and chose to live out the rest of her days in loneliness and isolation. Also, she never got a chance to see her family again as that would prove too dangerous both for her and them. So, you see, there were no winners here! Just absolute sadness and despair".

I don't know who the first girl was, but I know with all certainty that that was not me. For one, I lack her finesse, her confidence and her absolute purity. She is so regal that I feel like she has left some of that with me and I will carry it and pass it on to my children and their children will pass it on to theirs.

Having said all that needed to be said, all that could have been said, I run to my friends and we all run to the car and Nathan drives like the devil is after us to get the hell out of there.

Who ever that girl is, I know that she was and is a huge part of me. Even while we drove away from her, I could still feel her sadness, her unbearable sense of loss and her brokenness. I promised her that I would never become her and at that I felt her smile on my face.

Suddenly, I realized that this event might have been executed for all the wrong reasons but there was a knowing in my soul, that she had returned; however brief to inform me, that I should not become her. That I should fight with all my might and everything in me; to not become her, to not be that girl, who never allows herself to live out of fear. The one who never leaves her mark on the world through no fault of her own. She was a pawn in a very complicated game which no one won. There were no winners. How could there be? All the main players suffered unbearable loss. In that moment, I felt the deepest, most profound sense of loss and sadness that I have ever felt in my life.

Chapter 24

Shan

We get back to our hotel safely. Nathan goes to his hotel to get some stuff to stay with us for safety reasons. He sleeps on the couch, it is a little cramped but we all agree that it is for the good of the cause. I don't know if Kacia's little speech helped. I hope it does, if not for her then for the other young woman who the ancestors will select. Who knew homegirl was so brave to return to the scene of the crime. I am not sure if I would have been brave enough to do that.

My mind is still reeling from what aunt Toishma said – my aunt Toishma – I so love the sound of that. Can you imagine, having family that I didn't even know I had? I so wish I could go back and talk to her more and stay with her in the comfort of her little hut; no devices, no tv. Who knew a simple life could be so grand? I am so intrigued by what she said though and it makes perfect sense to me. My attraction to Nathan was too instantaneous and too magnetic and no wonder I couldn't stand Kacia.

There are so many mysteries to this world that might never be revealed; especially, on this continent which has kept so many of her secrets for centuries. Since I have been here, I have come to realize that this land is a living, breathing entity. Sometimes I can sense its vibrations; it is that intense. All ancestral lands are and if we truly listen, we will hear them speaking to us. The native Indians are well aware of this and so are other ethnic groups. This fully explains why when people are removed from their ancestral lands they feel, disconnected, misplaced, displaced – they lose focus – because that which both grounds them and sustains them has been unceremoniously removed. It is actually cool how our ancestors were able to locate both Kacia and myself. Naturally, our souls long for a place where we can call home – a place where our ancestors had roamed, a place where their sweat, tears and blood mingled. For me especially, nature has always been a huge part of who I am – a huge part of how I navigate planet Earth; therefore, without aspects of nature, I am rendered useless and ineffective.

Also, from time to time, my mind goes back to that great sense of loss suffered by my people. Every time, my mind goes back there, it hurts so much, it even hurts to breathe. There is absolutely no way to return everything that has been lost but I have a mandate now to live with a sense of dignity and reverence to honour my fore parents. I think of all the things lost, it is the reverence felt for each other great and small, a reverence for the land and a reverence of the old ways that is most missed by the ancestors. I am quick to note that it was not happiness or anything like that (which is not to say that happiness is not valued) but it is a communal reverence. Damn, I am never skipping Thanksgiving or Christmas at my mom's house again.

I am forever changed. I am forever grateful to my ancestors who have orchestrated this rendezvous with destiny. I got to meet my Lion, my prince, my sibling, my cousin; my what though? Who knows? I am eternally grateful though. I got to see apart of history unfold and meet my grand mother from a far a way place and time. We may never know exactly how we are connected to people but for sure our bodies have a way of informing us and whether we choose to investigate what our body says, is a completely other issue. This will definitely not be my last trip to the Mother Land.

Nathan

I am both Zulu and Xhosa! Talk about shocker! Don't get me wrong, I don't have beef with the Zulus, or being one but my whole identity so far has been premised on the fact that I am a Xhosa man. I even chose to live on Xhosa land. I guess in the scheme of things, that's not really a huge deal. Also, I am not old enough to have been affected by the struggles between the Zulu and Xhosa people in the past. I am

THEY WERE HERE BEFORE

still South African and that is the bigger picture. But why didn't anyone tell me sooner. Like really! EISH!

Moreover, I have never lived my life predicated on the whims of others. I have always sought to live in my own truth and be consistent in my pursuit of the truth. That being said, the events over the last few days have truly shaken me to my core. My core beliefs have always been to live in harmony with myself, those around me and follow the natural rhythm of life. I would like to think that I have been intentional in the way I have chosen to live my life and treat the people in my life. But now, I am no longer certain about what has been my truth as opposed to the path dictated by the ancestors or anyone else. In retrospect, how much of my life has actually been lived according to my own code of ethics? How much of it has been the wishes of the ancestors?

I certainly do have a lot to think about; especially, as it pertains to Kacia. With all due respect to the ancestors, I think I can find my way and choose my bride. Growing up, I was taught to honour the ancestors because of their contribution to my existence and because of their suffering, so I am conflicted in my assessment. Nevertheless, I would have preferred to have been left alone, to live my own life, at my own level of consciousness; to not be a scapegoat to be offered up as a sacrifice. The other thing I find quite perplexing is the knowledge that all my actions have been under surveillance from God knows when. Sweet Jesus! Anyways, what's done is done, and can not be undone. I just have to live with the awareness that all humanity is under constant scrutiny from one source or the next.

We, as in all three of us, have not really discussed the events that transpired last weekend. I really would like to talk to them though but I do not want to upset Kacia. She has been through a lot and although she is quite brave, it is a whole lot to process. I don't know if I would have returned to the market but anyways she felt a profound obligation to do it and I really hope that helped to appease my ancestors even a little bit. In retrospect, I think her life has been far more impinged on than mine so she has a whole lot more to assess and reconcile.

It is so much easier to talk to Shan, ever since we met, communication seems to flow between us, like the river into the sea; effortlessly, both verbal and non-verbal. I guess this confirms what auntie said that we are indeed kindred spirits, brought together by a shared ancestry.

On the other hand, Kacia has been a little more difficult to navigate. It is difficult to read her; however, to be fair she has been way more social and approachable over the last few weeks. But how much of that has been through the prodding of her ancestors? How much of those interactions have been about our natural connection? Do I really like her or do I feel obligated to accomplish the mandate of the ancestors? I have so many questions. Maybe, if she would just speak to me then I could be sure.

At any rate, I will just follow Kacia's lead. She is fiercely intelligent and unyielding in her quest for independence but she has suffered a tremendous trauma. A trauma which has never been documented so there is no frame of reference. So, at least for now, I will let it be, I will give her space to rest and resolve her own heart issues. One thing I know for sure, from past experience is that like a perennial plant, the heart heals, renews itself and returns with more wisdom and empathy, after a period of unrest.

They have another month before they return to the States, so I do have that on my side. Granted four weeks is not that long but according to ancient wisdom, the number four represents: loyalty, wisdom, trust, stability and justice. This might be a harbinger to great things ahead.

Kacia

I have always felt that I am paying for debts that I did not owe. I should have known that something otherworldly was at play. The truth is my mom always told me not to believe the lies being whispered in my ears because every lie is a twisted version of my truth. So very often, this world tried to beat me down to make me believe that I am nothing; therefore, I came to accept my nothingness and dressed my insignificance in a facade to hide my shame and pain. Meanwhile, I am a whole princess! Damn! I will never look at myself the same ever again. Do you know why? I took a beating in that village so every bruise, every scar, confirms my identity, validates my existence. Notwithstanding, not only the scars but also the horrific memories are confirmation of my place in the world, forever seared in my memory, like a birthmark. I don't know if Shan and Nathan believe any of what aunt Toishma

THEY WERE HERE BEFORE

said, but I believe every word. You best believe I believe every word. All these years I have accepted lies readily, almost eagerly; hence, I have learned how to detect the truth even while it's loading.

I have not yet discussed this with my friends but I suspect that they both know, even at a deeply repressed level that aunt Toishma spoke profound truths. Truths too deeply sacred for everyone in the universe to have knowledge of. We are beyond blessed to be part and parcel of the select few whose consciousness has been awakened to this monumental revelation.

We still have not yet discussed what happened. I know that eventually we will and it will not be a forced discussion, it will be organic. Those are the talks that I like because they are heartfelt. I hate forced conversation and the feeling that I am being patronized. One thing I know for sure, is that we will be having one of those rich conversations soon.

In the meantime, I do not know what will happen between Nathan and me but I am open to the possibility of a friendship and then we will see where it leads. I have learned my lesson well, I am therefore not going to give too much of myself too soon. Nathan did try to protect me many times, even in that dream when they were about to sacrifice me. Therefore, he has proven that he is a great guy so if we do end up being something special that would be awesome but I am not about to rush the process. I fully intend to give us time to come to terms with what has happened, and him time to choose of his own free will and volition, not just because the ancestors are pushy. God, they sure are pushy and here I was thinking that I have control issues. Meanwhile, he was being stalked. Plus, it is way too novel to make any decisions right now. Who knows, maybe I can both appease the ancestors and please my self in the process.

Chapter 25

Shan

The reports are complete, we spent days collecting data, interviewing people, fact checking and editing, we just need to hit submit. Everyone is super excited that we got everything done in "good time". Michael is thrilled. They are calling us the A-TEAM! State side, we are being praised for our efficiency here we are being congratulated for our attention to details, professionalism and compliance with industry standards. By all intents and purposes, this mission has proven to be a success. Everyone is happy except the three of us. Kacia has not mentioned a promotion not once over the last three weeks.

None of the three of us has mentioned the events in the craft market and at aunt Toishma either. Kacia has nightmares. Happy, Nathan and I are able to soothe her. I guess everyone is dealing with the fall out in his/her own way. I sense such deep sadness in Nathan. Sometimes I just want to give him a big hug but I don't want to make things more awkward than they need to be. Kacia has locked into herself. I can't read her at all. Every time I try, its access denied. She's a fighter though, so I know she will be fine! She is no longer the fake girl of the past either. We both have changed so much in such a short time.

The conclusion of the project means, I will have to go home and somehow continue to live as I did before, pretending as if I am the exact same person. But how could I still be her? The old Shan is gone. I didn't exactly hate her but I just prefer this new version of myself. I have experienced too much and still see a lot, to remain unchanged.

THEY WERE HERE BEFORE 87

Aunt Toishma was right, I am still having flashbacks from the past. Some of it is quite disturbing but I am learning to accept this as a part of my journey. It's like my eyes have been open to a whole new world that I didn't know existed and now I'm even more unsure of where I fit in the world. Is my place here in South Africa or is it in the USA? I am not sure of my new role in the world, now that I have a clear vision of the past. What is my new role and responsibility? I am only one person, I cannot change the world. I can only change how I interact with the world and allow it affect me. Maybe that's the lesson the ancestors are trying to teach me. That the past is the past and there is nothing that we can do about it, no going back to fix or change it. It's just there as a glaring reminder to all of us of exactly what we should not do. Also, to not allow my environment to dictate how I view myself or how I function in the world and that I should carve out a place for myself; instead of, waiting for a place to be made especially for me. To accept all my imperfections and be kind to myself, speak soothingly to myself like I would to anyone else.

With exactly a week left before we have to return to the States, Kacia and I have been running ragged, trying to get in every last bit of this beautiful place before we leave. Since neither of us knows when we will get a chance to return. We've been having breakfast, lunch and dinner at different restaurants; with Nathan as our able guide, just to sample all we can of the local cuisine. We've had Street food, market food, all types of fresh fruits and vegetables. How am I ever going to function in the US? We've been back and forth from Johannesburg and Pretoria taking in the sights: the Pretoria Museum was by far my favourite. We skipped the Lion And Safari Park. Nathan is the only lion I need to see in my world, thank you very much.   However, I found the Apartheid Museum in Joburg extremely overwhelming so we went to Gold Reef City Theme Park which was amazing. Nelson Mandela Square was cool too. So many things to see and do but so little time.

Over dinner last night, we managed to persuade Nathan to take us to the beach. This guy took us everywhere except the beach. I'm starting to think that he has some type of phobia. Each time we broach the topic, he quickly changes it. But last night, we were focused, united and determined so he could not say no. We've been rock climbing, we climbed mountains, we went wine tasting, to the Wild life Safari, twice: once in Pretoria and the other time in Joburg. We've done everything except go to the beach. Who goes to a country with hundreds of beaches and does not visit even one? Certainly not me!

Nathan decides to take us to his adopted home in Port Elizabeth, in the Eastern Cape. It's ten hours away so we decide to fly since we don't have much time left. The plan is, we will catch the early flight on Wednesday morning and return on the late flight on Friday so we can have two days to prepare to go home.

So, we get there and again we are stunned by the natural and architectural beauty of the city. We wonder aloud why we didn't stay here instead. But it's too late now. We go straight to Nathan's condominium, which makes my high-end apartment in NY look like the slums. Talk about luxury: two bedrooms, Mahoney furniture, modern kitchen, huge closets and a pool; plus, many other modern amenities. Also, he accidentally let it slip that he owns a beachfront home in another Province. Talk about living large on the down low. Once again, I marvel at his humility.

By the time we have dinner and settle in, it's raining heavily so going to beach is cancelled, a huge disappointment. However, according to the weather forecast, the next day looks great so Kacia and I are comforted.

Nathan still does not look thrilled. Does this mean he is missing us already? Is he still upset about the events which have transpired? What is it?

Kacia

After my supernatural encounter at the craft market, I couldn't wait to leave this God forsaken place. I threw myself into work and was pleasantly surprised to see that both Shan and Nathan are just as driven as I am and they rose to the occasion. We work exceptionally well together. Everyone giving one hundred and fifty percent of themselves daily, ten hours a day, five days a week. Sometimes, depending on the excursion that Nathan plans, we work weekends as well. No one complains. Every night we all crawl into bed dead tired. I don't know if working ourselves to the bone is our way of dealing with the trauma

THEY WERE HERE BEFORE

that we all shared; especially me, but it is not working. Despite being so tired, I still waking up screaming sometimes but I have my friends to soothe me when that happens. I've accepted that I might be having those nightmares for years to come but I know for certain that I am a survivor so I will be fine.

I am happy no one has brought up the event. I guess we are all still processing what has happened. Poor Nathan, he grew up thinking that he was one thing, only to discover over the course of a night, that he was something else all along. No gradual build up to the big reveal. Sometimes I catch him looking off into space. Who can blame him? I am pretty sure he will be fine, he has the spirit of a Zulu warrior in him so for sure he will overcome. Our people have been through hell and high water and survived. We all will survive and not only survive but thrive. Plus, Nathan has aunt Toishma to guide him. I guess we've all learned new things about ourselves. I am just as happy to leave it in the past until I can allow myself to revisit what happened and deal with it accordingly. I have accepted that I am a new person though. The old me is gone and I am not bitter. I am not stuck! I am not filled with self hate anymore. I am just accepting who I am and loving who I am. Also, I am not waiting on any man to rescue me and show me my worth, I am doing that all for myself and with the help of God I will be who I am meant to be.

I am really going to miss Nathan though.

Anyways, I was more than happy to leave and never look back until Nathan brought us to his home in Eastern Cape. I have never known such peace until I stepped off that flight in Port Elizabeth and the beauty of the city took my breath away. I felt like I was home, finally home. I don't know what has transpired but I feel like a weight left my shoulder.

Turns out that after supper it was raining so we couldn't go to the beach, I was a bit disappointment because we only have a few days to play with. Why did we leave this for the last minute? We've done everything else. I don't know when I fell asleep that night and I slept like a baby. Absolutely no nightmare. They had to wake me up so I could have breakfast and a quick shower before heading out to the beach.

Nathan

The ladies are leaving soon, so I can not put off taking them to the beach any longer. I probably should just tell them of my water phobia but I can't. Each time I try my mouth goes dry and my palms get wet. Plus, they both look so excited, like little kids, I feel bad to have to tell them that I can't take them because I am afraid. They've been through so much, the least I can do is accommodate them this last time. Who knows when we're going to see each other again! You know what, I am going to buy a whistle for each of us, so that we can signal for help if there's any trouble. Yes that's a good idea!

I am the man here! I shouldn't be so fearful. I can't forget that two times Shaney had to rescue me back there in the village even in my own dream; she was the hero. That's truly embarrassing. What kind of Zulu man am I, allowing a little water to paralyze me with fear? Anyways, today is the day, there's no going back from here. I am going to face my fear, sink or swim.

Chapter 26
A Day at the Beach

Shan

We are finally at the beach. But all my excitement has been replaced by a sense of foreboding that I've not felt in a long time. Even Kacia looks kind of out of it. I guess it's all the excitement and the build up, now that we are here, it's anti-climatic.

Nathan decided to take us to a private beach, one of those off the beaten path. It is so lovely, so inviting, the water is perfect, the sand is super white, the sky is clear and a striking blue, the sea birds are singing their song and the wind is still. However, something feels off though. I keep having a feeling that I've been here before which is not possible. Something is very wrong here!

Eventually, Kacia and I jump in, after all that is why we are here. Nathan is still hanging out on the shore. He keeps saying, "I'll join you ladies in a bit". But so far, he's a no show. Eventually, after much prodding, I see him coming towards us. We both start to clap, cheering him on like cheerleaders, but as soon as he enters the water, something weird happens.

Immediately, the sea becomes wild and vicious, the wind picks up and the waves grow boisterous. The sudden change takes us off guard-crippling our defences, there was no subtle build-up, no warning, just a swift, startling, savage shift. The waves seem like very angry soldiers who are trying to push us back to shore but their force has the opposite effect. Also, the quiet peace of the moment is interrupted by the growling of the sea, even the seabirds are quiet.

I see sheer panic in Nathan's eyes. I am trying to reach him but the waves keep pulling me back. Suddenly, it dawns on me that Nathan can't swim. Shit! Shit! Shit! I look across at Kacia and all I see in her eyes is real terror. She keeps going under but I can't reach her. Nathan is flailing. He is trying to save Kacia but in his hysteria, he is hitting the water too hard which is obviously counter productive. I can't save both of them. At this rate, there is no saving any of them. In that moment, I have to decide whether to sacrifice myself or save myself. There is no one around to help us; even the birds and the sun have disappeared. The sun hides behind the clouds as if to avoid witnessing our demise. I am so scared I can hear my heart beating in my ears like a drum.

I try to tell Nathan to go back so I can focus on saving Kacia but he is not paying attention. All his attention is fixed on saving her. I can hardly keep my head above water. I think I am going to die here.

All of a sudden, I have a very vivid memory of my dream from about three months ago. Now all the missing parts, which evaded me fall into place. Great! Just wonderful! It is now that I remember myself drowning, in a scenario exactly like this one!

I try to centre myself by thinking of the trees and the mountains, it is working and I am becoming calm. But all of a sudden, the past merges with the present and suddenly there is a huge ship docked at a small harbour. There are many people there; primarily, Black people, shackled to each other, mostly young women and sturdy young men. Time has stood still. I am floating above the water so I have an aerial view. Intuitively, just like before, I know what is happening. We are at a port where they previously sold and trafficked Africans to the new world to be kept as slaves. I see all the atrocities that will befall those who are taken.

In my mind there is a profound knowing, an ancient knowledge: that so many people chose to die here; instead, of being swept away to lands unknown. And again, that deep sense of sadness, that unfathomable sense of loss. It is unbearable! I am crying - no wailing, a deep guttural sound - for all the families shattered, all the lives ruined, all their potential destroyed, the dreams left unaccomplished; hanging in oblivion as if silently waiting for the owners to master them. They are

THEY WERE HERE BEFORE

adrift at sea and confused, unaware over the centuries that they are no longer bound to time and space. They don't know of the amelioration and abolition of slavery. They have been waiting all these years, at the point of transition, for someone to bring news of their liberty. They've been waiting here all this time for little, old me.

The sea became rough in the present because they don't know and they prefer to kill the three of us rather than allow us to be removed from our homeland. Rather than allowing us to suffer the torment of the unknown. They are trying to protect us!

All of a sudden, just like Kacia, I know what I have to do. I start off quietly but they can't hear me over the sea and the noise, so I have to shout I say, "My name is Shaney and I come from America". I realize that I am speaking an ancient language that I have never learned. A few of them start to pay attention but that's not enough. I remember that I have my safety whistle around my neck, so I blow it hard. That startles them and I feel their fear all the way in my bones, but at least I have their attention.

I continue through tears and a weakness that I have never felt ever:

I am the off spring of your ancestors. The ones snatched from Africa. I came back to tell you that the danger has past! You don't have to be afraid anymore. You don't need to protect us anymore. We are free now! Your siblings, cousins, my ancestors fought a hard battle for their liberty and they won. They won in the Caribbean and they won in the Americas. We are no longer slaves. We are free men and women with our destiny in our own hands. Free to act in our own best interest. There is no more lord and master, with whips above us. We even had a Black president in America – Barack Obama, was the forty fourth president. You guys also had a great, great, great, great, great grandson, Nelson Mandela – they called him Madiba – and he became South Africa's first Black president. Since then, there have been many, all Black.

I feel a few of them hovering next to me, touching my hair, my hands and my face – to see if I am real and truly one of theirs. I look down and I see them all laughing, hugging, clapping, crying happy tears. The shackles are breaking. Shackles can no longer hold them captive against their will. And just like that, they begin to disappear, one by one, waving good bye. I no longer feel that deep sadness anymore,

I feel relief.

Instantaneously, I am back in the present, the sea is calm and somehow Nathan got to rescue Kacia. He got to be her hero this time. He is holding her close to him like a child. He actually got to her and protected her from the winds and the waves. They are both smiling radiantly. When we return to shore, it is Nathan who breaks the silence. He looks scared, relieved and confused all at the same time.

"What the hell just happen here? Why is it always something with you guys? A brother could lose his life, just by hanging out with you two. Like what the fuck?"

Kacia and I laugh so hard we are rolling in the sand. He joins us after a while.

After we are able to breathe again, he says, "Are you guys ready for lunch because I am starving?"

I interject, "Almost dying will do that to you, every time!"

Kacia says, "I could eat!"

We start laughing again! I feel like a great weight has lifted from us and we can literally breathe again. We are laughing not just for ourselves, but we are laughing in the exact place where the tears of our ancestors flowed freely. Unwittingly, we have accomplished what we came here to do. We were able to set the spirits of our ancestors free by informing them of a truth that they could not have known.

Nathan is serious again, very serious. He demands, "Shan has a lot of explaining to do, because I don't know for sure what just happened but I know for sure something did. I actually swam today and that has never happened before".

For sure, I am going to have to share this experience with them this time. I know they felt it because I experienced it and since we are all connected, the experience resonated with them. Somehow, I know that they are ready to hear. This is going to be a very long and deep conversation. To think that before I came here, I was starved for deep, rich meaningful conversations. Well, it doesn't get more thought provoking than what I am about to share. I suspect that Nathan has a tale of his own to share about his fear of the water.

All this time, the ancestors were trying to protect him, us; after all, they were here before.

Acknowledgement

A huge thanks to all the people who have encouraged me and fed my creativity, I am eternally indebted to you. But more specifically, thank you to my husband and my children for their patients while I write and to my friend Tashna Servis Morris for your time and words of encouragement. Thanks to my parents who ignited a passion and deep love of books in me from very early by consistently saying, "go read you book", I took their advice literally and now I spend most of my spare time reading. My sister in law Marva Samuels, thank you for sharing my love of reading and all the books you've loaned me over the years. I really appreciate every single one of you; much love.

Lightning Source UK Ltd.
Milton Keynes UK
UKHW051255220820
368606UK00030B/968